PruDence

◆

Kayleigh Greer

For my husband, Jeremiah.

ProLoGue

December 2018

H er mind was fuzzy and she could hardly see through her sore, tired

eyes. The room was so bright that the detective seated in the chair

across from her was nothing but a dark silhouette engulfed by the white

walls behind him.

She couldn't hear what he was saying. For some reason, his voice was

muffled, as if she were in a glass box and he was trying to speak to her

through it. From time to time, she made out a few sentences as he

spoke. Like, "You have been read your rights," "We found her in your

apartment," and "Would you like a lawyer before we proceed?" She vaguely shook her head "no" to this, her brain sloshing between her ears as she did.

She knew what she had done and had no desire to fight whatever they had in store for her.

"Are you sure that you would like to waive your right to an attorney, Ms. Malkin?" asked the detective, peering at her over his spectacles, beads of sweat trickling to the end of his pointed nose.

"Prudence," she replied.

"I'm sorry?"

"You may call me Prudence," she answered, growing still again to watch as small strands of hair flew away then fell back in her face, her breath pushing against them.

The detective studied her motions for a time. It was as if watching this simple action brought her some minor amusement. He wasn't sure whether he should be repulsed by her indifference or astounded by it.

"Well, *Prudence...*" he began, "You do understand that this isn't just a traffic violation we're dealing with here. We found a woman in your apartment, stabbed to death, sitting in a pool of her own blood. This is murder we're talking about." He spoke boldly and expected that his words would cause her to stir in her chair, but she was not moved. She continued watching the few strands of hair rise and fall, rise and fall. After a beat or two, Prudence looked back up at the detective. She watched beads of sweat form on his brow and top lip. Only then did she notice how stuffy it was in the little, bright room. Prudence blinked a few times. Her eyes stung at the presence of moisture.

"I understand and, with clarity of mind, I can plainly say that I don't want an attorney. The crimes that have been committed tonight were done so by me and no one else and I shall be punished by the State of Maine for them. Would you like me to make my plea now?"

The detective froze, his mouth slightly agape, in awe at her response. It was not a common occurrence for a person to come into this particular room, sit in that chair, and say with such ease and eloquence that they were guilty.

He had to have been in this room hundreds of times over the course of his career and he had witnessed countless responses to this type of questioning. Never was "calm" a reaction he received. False serenity and indifference, yes, but he could always see through those who tried to feign ease in this situation, whether it was through their eyes or the amount of sweat that seeped from every orifice of their bodies.

Prudence   6

However, there was something unnatural about *Prudence*. She was in
her late 20s, he gathered from her report. Her eyes were the color of
dark chocolate and as deep as its flavor; sure to captivate and entrance
any poor fool. Her skin was the color of toasted almonds and her lips
were plump. An otherworldly beauty he would never have imagined
could be so calculated and vicious.

His voice cracked as he tried to speak but the words didn't form past
this. He rubbed his bald, sweaty scalp with his fingertips and sighed
deeply before straightening the papers that lay sprawled across the
small table between them. He grabbed his pen.

"First, *Prudence*, we'll need your statement."

"Very well," she said without adjusting in her seat for comfort. The
detective pushed his glasses back up on his nose, placed the voice
recorder closer to her, looked down at the papers, and began to write.

"It was late this afternoon when I arrived at my apartment, at
approximately 5 o'clock. I opened the door and walked inside. Moments
later, a knock sounded on my door. It was my landlady, Gretchen Hale. I
had been expecting this visit given the message she left on my cell
phone. I invited her in, offered her something to drink."

Prudence paused momentarily, getting her thoughts in line before she continued. Her heart beat gently, fluttering helplessly beneath what felt like a weight on her chest. Desperate to be free.

"There was no confrontation, no trading of foul language of any sort. I went to the kitchen with the intention of returning with a glass of water for Gretchen and the money order for my rent, which she had initially come by to collect. Instead, I came back into the dining room with a knife from the block in my kitchen. It was a nine-inch blade, I believe, two and a quarter inches wide. I stabbed her on the left side of her neck at a diagonal. Then I retrieved the knife and proceeded to slit her throat. She slumped over in her chair and began to bleed out. I walked around the chair to the front of her and stabbed her numerous times in the chest and abdomen. I lost count after 30. I murdered the late Ms. Gretchen Hale, and I'm prepared to face the penalty for said crime."

Once she was finished, Prudence sat without blinking and awaited his response.

The detective removed his glasses and rubbed his eyes. He couldn't believe this woman. She had been so calm and detached as she described the gruesome nature of her crime. Unphased, immovable, just

still. He would have thought her cold had it not been for the muggy air
around them.

The detective rolled up his sleeves and clasped his hands together on
the table between them.

"And what was the reason, Prudence? I mean, why kill a 57-year-old
woman in cold blood?" he asked, his eyes searching hers for something,
anything, to help him understand.

Her eyes narrowed, "I don't believe the reasoning behind the killing is
relevant, detective."

"But—"

"You will have your guilty plea. Coupled with the evidence you have,
there is nothing more, *technically*, that you need to move forward with
this investigation."

"Ok, ok... You've made yourself quite clear, Ms. Malkin—sorry,
Prudence."

"So," she began. "What now?"

CHAPTER 1

It didn't take the judge long to sentence Prudence, due in part to how

adamant she was to move the process along as quickly as possible. She

felt unbothered as the judge spewed his feelings of utter disdain for

what she had done and the manner in which she had done it. Her

temperament remained even through his monologue as she focused

more intently on a bird perched on the window sill just outside the

courtroom.

It was a plump robin, its red-feathered belly slightly pressed against the

glass as it struggled to turn its back to Prudence. It reminded her of a

beanie baby she had as a child. The cherished moments of serenity alone

in her room seeped into the forefront of her mind as she envisioned the little stuffed bird propped up in a small wicker basket placed beside her bed.

"Do I bore you, Ms. Malkin?" the judge erupted. Her brow twitched at the sharp sound his voice made when he proclaimed her surname so aggressively.

"Ever so slightly, your honor." Her gaze shifted away from the spot where the robin had flown away and toward the judge. She found a touch of humor in how he grumbled in response to her statement and writhed about in his seat.

"What do you have to say for yourself?" he spat as his face contorted and reddened.

Prudence looked away without answering.

"Well, if you have nothing to say for yourself, what do you have to say to Gretchen Hale's family? Hm? Any explanation as to why you took her from them?"

Prudence's stomach turned and her pulse quickened. "Family?" She heard feet hit the ground behind her, awakening all the sounds in the courtroom. Now she could hear sobbing, sniffling, muffled speech—none of which had reached her ears before.

It was the bird. She was too focused on the bird.

"Yeah!" a voice roared behind her. She turned to face it. "What do you have to say?"

Prudence's eyes fell upon a man of average height. She noticed his eyes were blistered red, no doubt from tears. A few people sat around him. In them, she could see Gretchen's beady eyes, Gretchen's bulbous nose, Gretchen's mousy brown hair.

"I—" Prudence's eyes stung, her mouth agape. She formed no words but still they waited for her response, for her answer, for her reason why. The many sets of Gretchen's eyes burned into her like a lit cigar to the skin. She bit her lip and turned away from them. "I hadn't any idea she had a family."

Her heart steadied once they were all out of her line of sight. Her ears once again grew deaf to their words as she resumed staring at the window sill.

The judge gave Prudence her sentence and ordered her out of his court. The bailiff took her by the arm and escorted her out. Despite the roaring applause behind her, all Prudence could think about was that she wished the robin had returned.

◆

Walking down the hall to her cell, between a pair of officers, Prudence could feel all eyes on her, but she remained unfazed. Some of the women in the cells that she walked past spat at her, made salacious remarks and the like—she didn't care.

The guards banged their batons on the cell bars to silence the inmates and threatened them with solitary confinement. Prudence couldn't help but smile at the thought of being in solitary confinement. To be thoroughly alone was all she had wanted from the moment this whole process began. She didn't imagine it would be terribly difficult to get such a privilege.

Three other new arrivals were escorted with her into a single cell where they would remain temporarily until they were assigned to a particular block. Each of them swiftly claimed a bunk for herself. Prudence climbed to the top bunk and unfolded the blanket she had been given. It was thin and lacked the ability to insulate well, but it would do. When she laid her head on the flat pillow, a grainy, stale fragrance immediately filled her nose.

Her companions started to socialize the moment the cell door was closed and locked, but Prudence was uninterested in their pointless conversation. Instead, she closed her eyes and forced their voices to drain from her ears until she was left with silence. Unfortunately, with that silence came the resurgence of the sounds from that night.

The shrill sound of Gretchen's voice coming through the door as she knocked. The unsheathing of the knife from the block. The gurgling sounds Gretchen made as blood gushed from her neck.

Prudence's own labored and controlled breathing.

This replay of sounds wasn't so much distressing for Prudence as it was tiresome. Her mind wouldn't rest. So, she hummed a song she had known her entire life as she let her muscles relax into the thin, stiff mattress. The tune stifled the sounds in her mind.

CHAPTER 2

The fluorescent lights in the cell came on with a loud surging sound

that quieted to a soft buzz. Prudence woke to this and the sound of her

cellmates groaning in protest. The guards walked past their cell,

announcing that it was time to "rise and shine."

"Breakfast will be served in one hour. You ladies have until then to rub

the sleep out of your eyes and get down there. It's first come first

served, so if there ain't shit left for you to eat, don't come crying to me,"

said a guard just outside their quarters. Prudence assumed he did this as

a courtesy so that they would be aware of the way things worked here.

Nice but not very subtle. His voice was reminiscent of that of the officer

who had escorted her to her cell but she couldn't see him to be sure.

That particular guard, she noticed, wasn't quite as stern as the others.

Though he barked, she could tell his bite wouldn't pierce the skin.

"Gallagher," his name badge read.

She made her way into the showers alongside the other women with the
care package that all the new arrivals received. It contained a small set
of shampoo and conditioner, a bar of soap, toothpaste, and a terribly
flimsy toothbrush. It had been days since she'd been able to shower.
Prudence stood and waited anxiously in line for a stall to become
available.

Suddenly, a woman behind her tapped her shoulder. Prudence didn't
react, not even a flinch to acknowledge that she had felt the presence of
the other inmate. She hadn't entertained anyone thus far and was not
interested in starting now. The woman spoke a few words, trying to gain
her attention, and even made mention of how she liked the way
Prudence's backside was perfectly shaped but still Prudence didn't
engage.

"Whatever, bitch. You're ugly anyway," she said finally.

Prudence snickered, "It would seem not."

"Excuse me?"

Prudence turned to face the woman, an eyebrow raised, and plainly stated that if the woman found no interest in her, she wouldn't have bothered trying to make a pass in the first place.

"Ha! You think you're hot shit, don'tcha?" The woman leaned in closer. "I bet that mouth can do more than just talk nice." Prudence grimaced at the foul scent of the woman's breath. The ladies around them began murmuring amongst each other, giggling at what they assumed would become a fight.

"You won't be finding that out anytime soon," Prudence said, turning away from her and stepping forward in line. Her attention had been caught by a vacant stall. Due to the missing shower curtain, she had no doubt that it was empty.

The giggling grew into full-on laughter. Just when Prudence began making her way toward the available stall, the woman jerked her around and punched her in the face.

Prudence didn't react, didn't get angry. She wiped the blood from her nose with the back of her hand and walked into the stall.

"Come at me, you uptight bitch!" the woman roared at the back of her head but Prudence couldn't be swayed. Her sole interest was in taking a shower to wash away the film of grime that had set in from previous

days—and now the blood that seeped from her nose.

By now, the walls of the bathroom vibrated with loud chanting: "Fight!

Fight!"

An officer was standing just outside the women's shower room when

the commotion caught his attention. He pushed through the crowd of

inmates and pulled Prudence's attacker to him when he noticed her

bloodied hand.

"That's your second shot, Collins. One to go."

"Fuck you, Kore. This cunt over here started it," she growled, pointing

to Prudence, who was now naked under the shower. Officer Kore

watched as she washed the blood away and cradled her nose tenderly.

"Inmate!" His voice boomed to get her attention. Prudence's closed

eyes came open, her jaw tensed, and her brow rose in annoyance.

"Problem, sir?" she asked without sparing a glance at Officer Kore.

"You've earned yourself a shot for this spat with Collins. What's your

name?" he ordered, still holding a firm grip on Collins. The chatter from

the other women grew. He unsheathed his baton and slammed it on the

sink beside him to silence them.

"Prudence."

"Last name, inmate," he demanded, his voice deepening.

Finally, she looked in his direction, told him it was '*Malkin*', and looked away. She closed her eyes and hoped that now she could just enjoy the sensation of water cascading down her tired body in peace.

Officer Kore felt a chill in his spine at the vacant look in her eyes when she gazed at him, the acidic tone in her voice as she uttered her name. He didn't find it particularly difficult to contain his sense of uneasiness around the inmates but this one, regrettably, made him feel anxious.

"A few more shots and you'll be in solitary, too," he warned. Then, with one more glance at her, he escorted Collins out. Once he made it around the corner, he felt like he could finally exhale.

"She had some nice tits, huh, Kore?" Collins snickered, sensing the tension in his shoulders subside.

"Shut up or else three strikes, you're out."

"Oh my God!" The woman in the neighboring shower stall peered around the corner at Prudence. "You showed her! She's always trying to start something." She was practically standing in the stall with Prudence now, stark naked. Prudence made an effort not to look at her but she instinctively glanced at the woman when she noticed her drawing too near. She had rather small breasts for the astounding size of her pink nipples.

Prudence found herself grimacing again.

"With all due respect, if you'd remove yourself from my shower, please..."

"Oh! Yeah, sorry!" She sheepishly made her way back into her stall.

"I'm Berkeley, by the way. Was nice talkin' to you."

Through breakfast, all Prudence could think about was what she could do, while also causing minimal harm to herself, that would qualify her for "solitary," as Officer Kore put it. For now, it was easy to block out the other inmates but she knew she would grow tired of constantly being in close proximity to them. She knew she'd need time alone if she was going to make it in here without succumbing to her psychosis. Regrettably, starting fights seemed to be the easiest way to do so. Still, she was eager to have received her first "shot," bringing her closer to what she desired.

Looking down at her tray, Prudence mashed her oatmeal with her plastic fork until it was spread evenly in its little rectangular compartment. She nibbled on a sweet bun and drank a cup of black coffee that more closely resembled muddy water. She couldn't stomach much more. Her nose, though the bleeding had stopped, was sore and throbbing. She'd glanced at her appearance in the mirror before leaving the shower room and noticed that it had swelled slightly, though the bruising was minimal. This wasn't the first time she had been punched in the face and it wasn't nearly the worst she had received. She wagered it would take about a week before it was back to normal.

"Peaches?" a voice sounded. Prudence could see the waist of an orderly standing in front of her.

She paused, her brows crossing as she set down her fork and looked up at the man's face. She caught a glimpse before immediately looking away, then sighed audibly.

How could I possibly be this unlucky?

The man walked around the table and bent down to meet her gaze. The familiar scent of his cologne filled her nose, making her nauseous. "Tsk, tsk, Peaches. What have you done?"

"Edgar, I—" Before she could continue with her statement, he silenced her by slamming his palm on the table, rattling her tray but not Prudence. She rolled her eyes and popped each of her fingers under the table before looking back up at him.

"Officer Benitez, inmate." He spoke sternly, almost aggressively.

"Hm." She smirked. "I wasn't privy to your profession, Officer Benitez. How noble."

A low chuckle built in his chest as he stood up straight. Her eyes followed him up. He was the kind of handsome that most women were smart to steer clear of. Edgar was the definition of "narcissist," with a permanent smug smile on his face that made her eyes roll. It truly was a shame that she couldn't just as easily erase him from her life as she'd done with all the other men she had encountered in the past.

"That it is. Not everyone is fit to regularly discipline a herd of bitches such as these. I'm sure you remember very well how I *disciplined* you." He adjusted his manhood directly in front of Prudence's face. At his words, bile and bits of sweet bun rose in her throat.

"I'm sorry, did you come over here to reminisce or is there something you actually needed to tell me? Because if it's nothing, I'd much rather prefer to continue having my breakfast free of pork..."

"You mean to tell me I didn't satisfy you? Your trembling thighs and throbbing pussy told me otherwise," he remarked loud enough for the surrounding inmates to hear. The smug look on his face somehow intensified. "I wondered why I didn't hear from you after, you know, for seconds. But now I see why."

Prudence matched his smug look with that of indifference. She pushed away from the table and stood up to him.

"I just needed to fuck. Your cock was no doubt exceptional but I was fully satisfied and returned to my senses. I no longer had a use for you."

Edgar grabbed her arm and pulled her to him. By now, whispering started to swarm around the cafeteria as more took notice of Edgar and Prudence. His scent was intense, bringing back the memory of her being beneath him; it was thoroughly repelling.

He said, "We'll see about that. After too long, they all give in and come begging for it."

She jerked away from him, grabbed her tray, and took it to the trash can. Prudence couldn't fathom eating after such a conversation. She was unsettled, not only because of the insurmountable number of women he must have fucked at this facility but mostly because she knew he was right. She was repulsed by him now but she knew that when her impulses arose, she would need a release again.

"Hey, Malkin!" A cheerful voice sounded over her shoulder. Berkeley, with her bouncy bobbed hair jumping about her face, discarded the contents of her tray and set it on top of the trash can after Prudence.

"Prudence," she corrected before attempting to walk away.

"Oh, sorry. We usually go by last names here. B–but I don't mind callin'
you Prudence!" Berkeley spoke as she followed close behind. "I seen you
was talkin' to Benetiz. He's such a sleaze. You oughta be careful around
him," she said, rubbing her arm sheepishly.

Prudence rolled her eyes at this. Berkeley didn't know the half of it.

"Where you headed?"

"Why does that concern you?" Prudence replied.

"Was just wonderin'…you wanna hang out? Maybe?" she asked,
quickening her pace to keep up with Prudence, to no avail. "I'm kinda
new here too, thought it'd be nice if we could be friends."

"To be completely transparent, uh…What was your name again?"

"Berkeley!"

"*Berkeley*. I don't hang out nor do I have the desire to, no matter how
benevolent you may be."

Prudence turned the corner and strolled into the library, not holding the
door for Berkeley to follow. Berkeley hesitated, her fingers knotting
together as she contemplated following despite Prudence's response.
She didn't want to upset Prudence but she also didn't want to be alone
in this place anymore. She felt, even if this was the only benefit to

forging some kind of bond with her, Prudence would be the one to keep everyone at bay.

Berkeley possessed all the features of the wrong type of person to be incarcerated. She'd been sentenced to five years of imprisonment for smuggling marijuana across the US/Canadian border. Her boyfriend had convinced her it would be no big deal.

He was wrong.

She was fragile, impressionable, and timid. Like a beacon, these characteristics were very apparent to the other inmates. Berkeley had been bullied and kicked around, and she'd dealt with advances from Collins that she was certain she couldn't avoid forever. Judging by her handling of that rift with Collins, Berkeley could tell that Prudence was someone she wanted on her side.

Summoning up just enough gumption, Berkeley walked into the library after her. Prudence was walking up to a table in the small makeshift library, a hardback in hand. As she took her seat, unaware of Berkeley's presence, Berkeley quickly slid into the seat in front of her.

"Look, I heard what you said," Berkeley began.

Prudence didn't spare her a glance as she cracked open her book.

"But could I just maybe sit with you? Like now or durin' rec time or at lunch sometimes?"

Prudence still didn't respond, making Berkeley feel like she was talking to herself. She knotted her fingers, elbows on the table. "I don't mind if you don't talk back, neither."

"You can sit there, quietly, if that's what you choose to do but be aware that I won't engage past this statement."

Prudence turned the page of her book and began to read Leo Tolstoy's "War and Peace" as Berkley sat with her in silence.

CHaPTer 3

March 2019

He dreamt about her that night, and many of the nights following.

Vincent couldn't stop thinking about Prudence Malkin and didn't quite understand why she was having such an effect on him. After all, she was a new inmate, like many before her, but something about her drew him in.

In the days following their initial meeting in the women's shower room, Vincent had actively avoided her, fearing that he wouldn't be able to uphold his authority over her.

She had a peculiar air that gave off the distinct impression that she was not to be controlled and wouldn't be easily frightened. He had noticed the light in her eyes when he mentioned solitary confinement to her as a threat. She seemed excited about the thought of one of their harshest punishments. If that were the case, what could he truly threaten her with without stepping out of his bounds as a responsible officer of the law? She had no names on her visitation list, so it wasn't as if he could threaten her with limited visitation. Nor, after reading her court record, could he imagine she'd mind being given more time on her sentence, considering she had practically shrugged when being sentenced.

She was, it seemed, without restrictions.

Vincent lived alone in a one-bedroom studio apartment with his pug, Broccoli, whom he affectionately called Brocc for short. Brocc was a great distraction for getting Prudence off of his mind at times. Taking him on walks and playing took up a good deal of Vincent's time but Brocc was also a damn good listener. So, when Vincent felt too engulfed by thoughts of Prudence, Brocc became his soundboard. At times, he felt like Brocc was getting tired of hearing about her but Vincent was relieved that the poor pup couldn't talk back. Couldn't tell him to shut up, move on, and get over himself. He was especially relieved that Brocc couldn't tell him that it was crazy to develop romantic feelings for an inmate.

Vincent knew of other orderlies—several, actually—who did partake of the forbidden fruit. He was always disturbed by it and couldn't fathom how they could get past how morally wrong it was. The idea of sleeping with a criminal, never mind the fact that it was illegal, was astoundingly atrocious to him. But here he was, with Prudence plaguing his every thought.

He was beginning to question his own morality.

Vincent scratched the stubble on his chin as he mulled this for the hundredth time. Usually, he spent his time in traffic listening to podcasts about history or fantasy-based game play but lately he had been spending it deep in thought. Finally, his lane started to roll at a more consistent pace and he began to focus more on the road. Maine in March felt much like it did in December, with its freezing temperatures and blistering winds coming off the coast. Even this late, the roads were still relatively clear; all the snow built up from the night before had long since been pushed up off the roads by the early morning snow plows. Beige mountains of ice lined the streets. Vincent had spent most of his only day off running errands and was ready to relax but didn't want to go home right away. He had to distract himself for a little while, so he called Gallagher to join him.

He turned on the radio and tuned into one of the various shows he liked, trying to get Prudence off his mind. Despite the presence of sound in his ears, the thought of her persisted in drowning it out. His mind wandered to her soul-incinerating eyes and the water cascading down her naked body. Vincent's mind was trapped by unrelenting replays of his first image of her. She was striking, to say the least, with her taut, plump breasts and full, shapely hips. Blood rushed vigorously through his veins as he sighed heavily.

He lasted a week of avoidance before he decided it was best to request a change in department.

"Solitary? Why would you want to move to solitary?" Warden Seifert asked him when Vincent formally put in his request.

"Change of scenery," Vincent said. "I've been in the mix for almost three years now. I think a little quiet will be good for me."

"Oh, it's not always quiet. There's bound to be one or two who start howling after the loneliness sets in." Seifert chuckled his ashy chortle.

"One inmate howling is still substantially quieter than the hundreds I hear every day, sir," he replied, smirking slightly.

"Ha! If that isn't true!" Seifert laughed again, "Alright, Kore. We'll shuffle something around. Should take effect in, well, maybe a week's time. Just keep in mind, these women can get pretty crafty when they become desperate. Fletcher will give you the rundown when the time comes."

The warden's last words echoed in his mind.

In his first few days, Vincent could see exactly what he was talking about in the way the women spoke to him with bribes of sexual acts if he allowed them a little extra time out of their cells. Vincent was accustomed to women hitting on him. It didn't elude him that he was a good-looking man. His tawny brown hair and beard were thick and well kept. His eyes were crystal blue and he towered over most men. But the attention he got in solitary was unfounded. It was sad and terribly humbling to see these women in such a state of desperation. Craving human contact of any kind, practically going mad without it. However, even after he'd spent three weeks in solitary pitying these women, *she* hadn't escaped his mind, not even briefly.

Still, it was easier to work when he didn't see Prudence Malkin anymore. He parked his car on the side of the street and pulled his emergency brake. With inclined streets like these, slick from ice and snow, he knew to take every precaution. Vincent jammed his hands into his pockets for warmth as he made his way up the cobblestone street and around the corner to Gritty's.

Gritty's was a small pub on Fore Street in Old Port. Its sign was a dim version of what it once was but people were still drawn to it like a beacon after work. Here they could drown the sorrows and frustrations of the day. On the wall behind the bar, trailing up and onto the ceiling, was a display of beer mugs reserved for the most loyal patrons. It smelled of old wood and the furnishing itself was so over-stained by the spills of drink after drink that none of them were their original color. It was a pub pure and true, with patrons from many backgrounds—from business-clad men to an older man with a mohawk and a walking stick with a doorknob glued to its tip. Many of the orderlies from the women's prison, which wasn't far away, made their way in most nights and boasted loudly about the bullshit they put up with for bullshit pay. Vincent was no stranger there. The bartender, Phil, would always pull down his personal mug and fill it with his favorite Black Fly Stout when he saw Vincent come in on most Saturday nights. Gallagher was already seated at the bar top, with several other guys from work surrounding him, as Vincent walked up to claim his mug.

Joe Gallagher was his closest friend—a short, stocky, jubilant man who was a perfect contrast to Vincent's tall, broad frame and more stern demeanor. They'd met almost a decade ago when Vincent was in his second year of college. Gallagher was a few years older than him so, naturally, he'd taken Vincent under his wing like the big brother Vincent never had—even though Gallagher was almost a foot shorter than him. The greek god and his witty irish sidekick.

"Hey, man!" Gallagher's round face beamed at Vincent, breaking up the laughter no doubt onset by one of his numerous jokes.

"How's it going?" Vincent asked, taking his seat and grabbing his beer, winking at Phil as he did.

"Same shit, different day, ya know." He shrugged, taking a swig of his beer. Gallagher had opted for a Pilsner that night. He often flip-flopped between different styles of beer but grimaced at the bitter, almost black, stouts that Vincent enjoyed.

The perfect contrast.

Just as the first crisp gulp flowed down his throat, Vincent saw, in the corner of his eye, Edgar Benitez make his way through the crowd. Vincent cleared his throat and pretended he didn't see him. That steaming bag of garbage didn't just press buttons, he mashed them. He boasted about relations with the inmates, like he was some kind of deity

that had immense control over them because of his "golden cock."

Vincent despised Edgar for how he violated and disrespected the women

of the prison. Typically, Vincent avoided him when possible. Even if

they were inmates, they were still humans.

Not his sex slaves.

Vincent diverted his attention back to Gallagher, who was on another

roll of puns, causing a wave of laughter to wash over their group.

"I'm just saying! I'd take a million prostate exams in one week if that

meant I didn't ever get another used tampon thrown at me!" Gallagher

stood and started unbuckling his pants, "Alright, doc, warm up that

finger!" The crowd roared again.

Vincent laughed, patting Gallagher's arm to get his attention. "Would

you like to report an incident?" Gallagher snickered, taking his seat

again.

Before he knew it, Vincent had downed pint number three and was

taking the first sip of his next. He was feeling very good, relaxed, a buzz

stealthily creeping up on him.

"How's Brocc?" Gallagher asked. As the night went along, fewer of their

coworkers remained, leaving the two of them more time to talk.

Gallagher was nursing his current beer and munching on an order of fried pickles.

"Sick of me, ha!"

"Yeah?" He crunched on a pickle. "What you do?"

"Talking his ear off." Vincent took another generous gulp. He hadn't told Gallagher about his insatiable interest in Prudence and wasn't quite sure he was ready to admit it. This buzz was making his lips loose, however, and he was showing no signs of slowing down. Phil made his way back to their side of the bar and Vincent motioned for a fresh pint. Out of the corner of his eye, Gallagher saw Edgar trying to interject himself in a conversation between two women standing by the bar. They were polite when he approached them but were visibly uncomfortable with his presence.

"Look at him." Gallagher nudged Vincent's arm, almost causing him to spill his beer. "Couldn't take a hint if it smacked him in the face." Vincent looked up at Edgar, his loose lips separating. He watched him get closer to one of the ladies in particular, reaching around to grab her bottom. When his hand landed and squeezed, Vincent stood up and yelled, "Keep your damn hands to yourself, Benitez!"

Edgar raised both his hands in defense and the women scurried away.

"What's with the cock blockin', Vin?"

Vincent approached him, fury burning in his eyes. "They didn't seem interested."

"Come on, I was just foolin' around." Edgar's hands dropped to his sides, a cocky grin on his face, "Put your guns away, Chief." He patted Vincent on his arm and turned to walk away.

Heavily influenced by his fifth stout, Vincent grabbed Benitez by the shirt collar and started for the door.

"Whoa, Vin, buddy!" Gallagher followed behind, trying to grab Vincent's arm. He couldn't stop him. Vincent was at full throttle, charging through the door, dragging Edgar outside.

He flailed, to no avail. "What the fuck is wrong with you? I'll fuck you up, you goddamn Neanderthal!"

With one hand on his collar and the other firmly gripping his belt loop, Vincent tossed Edgar so hard that when he landed in the snow, he emerged with his face sliced up and bloody. It looked like he had gone through a window.

Edgar stood up and spit out a glob of blood, slurring profanities at the back of Vincent's head as he marched back into the pub and slammed the door.

Edgar was smart not to follow him back inside.

CHAPTER 4

February 1999

Last night was particularly brutal. Prudence rubbed at the tender

bruises on her wrist and tried desperately not to think about it. About

any of it.

She woke up today like she did on any other weekday, around 6:30 am, to

get ready for school. She wanted today to be a good day, to erase all the

bad of yesterday and so many days prior that were just like it. Her little

throat burned as she inhaled and exhaled, having spent all night crying.

Her nose was stuffy and her eyes were burning and red. Prudence sifted

through the clothing in her closet to find an outfit that would brighten and set the tone for the day. She had so many articles of clothing, from frilly blouses to dresses and skirts, fluffy from excessive layers of itchy tulle.

Mother and Father always bought her the prettiest things.

She came upon a butter yellow dress with long sleeves, as Mother instructed her to wear when she looked like *this*. The sleeves were frilly and, in the front, were fabric rosette buttons that drew up her neck like a row of yellow roses. Prudence's mouth flickered into a smile as she admired it.

It was so thoughtful and kind of Mother to have gotten me something so pretty. I just know she loves me.

As she dressed herself, every inch of her body ached and stung—so much so that tears started to stream down her face, but she stifled a sob. She wasn't going to exhibit pity for herself because, as she had learned over the last couple of months, it would only make things worse.

Once Prudence was dressed, and after double-checking her appearance in the mirror, she made her way to the kitchen, where mother usually waited for her with her vitamins and breakfast. But she wasn't there and neither was Father. "Mother?" Her little voice quaked slightly. She walked through the kitchen and down the hall to her parents' door. Fire boiling the acid in her empty tummy burned furiously as she summoned

the gumption to knock.

Mother sprang out from behind the door. "What? What do you want?"

"I—it's almost time for school."

"You're not going to school. Did you bathe?" her mother asked.

"But, Mother, it's Monday." Tears welled up in her eyes.

"You're not going back to that school! They ask too many questions

thanks to you." Her mother grabbed Prudence by the shoulder and

shoved her away from the door. "Go wash yourself, you *disgusting* little

girl!"

Prudence did as she was told and took a shower, even though she had

already taken one, scrubbing her skin vigorously until it reddened.

She lay in bed for what felt like hours, sobbing quietly into her pillow,

her pretty yellow dress becoming a wrinkled mess. She didn't

understand what was happening or why.

What had she done wrong?

Was she not covering up enough?

Was it wrong to tell the teachers she had fallen, as Father told her to?

All she knew was that she wanted to go to school, needed to, to get away. Even if just for a while.

Footsteps echoed through the house now that her parents were finally up. Prudence wiped her tears and made herself calm down, pushing her feelings and heartache down further and further each time.

Once her face was dry, she reached into her backpack and pulled out a "Junie B. Jones" book that she had checked out of the school library last week. She felt overwhelmingly glad that she still had it, her heart warming at the image of Junie on the cover in all her rambunctious glory. Prudence lay across her bed and flipped open the book to the page where she had left off. It was marked by a bookmark adorned with a curly "P" and a white tassel. She immersed herself in the world of the book, getting into shenanigans with Junie, playing dress-up in her mother's clothes. Prudence giggled at the pictures of Junie with her scrunched-up, freckled nose and bossy expression.

How Prudence longed to be as open and free as Junie was.

A song started to play. Its sound waves flowed through her door and into her ears, pulling her out of the book. It was *her* song, according to Father. "Because it's your name!"

When the song played, Prudence always felt a flutter in her heart, as it indicated that a good day was to come. The smell of pancakes reached her nose, causing her tummy to rumble loudly. She wedged her bookmark in the book to hold her place again and jumped from the bed. When she reached the kitchen, both of her parents were there. Father had a big grin on his otherwise ridgid face as he beckoned for her to dance with him. Prudence eagerly ran into his embrace, hugging him tightly as she glided around the kitchen, standing on top of his feet. Mother made her way to the table with a boat of warm butter pecan syrup in hand. She smiled at them as she finished setting the table. The song curled around Prudence's ears as she hummed along to the tune.

"Sorry about everything, Prue. Mommy and Daddy are just stressed," Mother said, taking her seat at the table. Today they were "mommy and daddy," which was also a very good sign.

Prudence giggled as father twirled her around and around before catching her in his arms. Her head and heart were dizzy with this onslaught of affection.

"It's ok!" she said, sitting beside Mother, who was now drenching her hot pancakes with the golden syrup. The song ended and a new one started. Father lowered the volume and took his seat as well. They each clasped their hands together and bowed their heads. As Father said grace, before diving into her tower of sweetness, Prudence prayed to herself that every day from now on would start with her song.

CHAPTEr 5

March 2019

Vincent shuffled a few things around in his locker, throwing out an old bag of unfinished pretzels and grabbing pieces of his uniform that he had purposely left there so Brocc wouldn't attempt to devour them when he wasn't looking at home. When he shut the locker door, Gallagher appeared from behind it, startling him. "Vin!"

"Hey," Vincent bellowed. "Shit, man, you scared me."

"A big fuck like you? Come on…" he scoffed. "You heard about Benitez?"

Vincent's lips thinned. "No, why?"

"He got fucked up!" Gallagher laughed. A few of the other orderlies gathered in the locker room murmured amongst each other about the same incident. Vincent heard one of them describe how swollen Edgar's face had gotten, "like he got stung by a giant hornet!"

"No shit? At Gritty's?" Vincent asked. A smirk crawled across his face as he reminisced about a few nights ago.

"No, not at Gritty's, but you're not going to believe it," Gallagher said, interrupting his train of thought. "You know that inmate Malkin? Been here like two months? She fucking headbutted him!"

Vincent's grin widened as surprise reached his eyes. Gallagher was laughing so hard, he could hardly breathe.

"What did he do?" Vincent inquired, pinning his nametag above his shirt pocket, feigning disinterest in having heard her name.

"Oh! Ha! Oh man, hold on!" Gallagher took a deep breath to gather himself. "No one knows, she just freaked. The inmates were sitting down for breakfast this morning when Dipshit made his way toward her and whispered in her ear—something nasty, I'm sure. She smiled and fucking headbutted him! Right in the nose! Then she grabbed her tray and POW! Hit him over the head, then SWOOSH! Bashed him in the knees, taking his feet right from under him! Ha-ha!" Gallagher was holding his side at this point. The orderlies around them were tuned into his telling of the story and were coming completely unraveled.

Vincent found himself laughing, too. "Well, is the bastard ok?"

"Oh yeah, he's fine. Taking a sabbatical for his *injuries.* Malkin was sent to solitary for a couple of weeks."

Vincent's stomach dropped.

Though that would be the obvious outcome for any of the inmates had they attacked an orderly, it didn't cross his mind that Prudence would now be in solitary with him.

◆

The first two days, she slept mostly.

He would look in on her to make sure she ate the food they provided, but every time he peeked in, she was lying down, facing the wall. Vincent studied her in this position for a time. She looked so peaceful. Serenity clearly found her in solitude and he was practically feeding off her energy, feeling a calmness within himself as he watched her. Prudence was draped in a thin blanket, her legs pulled up to her chest. Her tight, dark—almost black—curls rested on the bed, sprawled out behind her like hot molasses.

Gertrude Turner, the officer who monitored the solitary cells during the day shifts, told Vincent that Prudence would respond when spoken to, but simply wouldn't eat much.

"Maybe it's a hunger strike," she said.

"It's not a hunger strike if she's still eating," he replied, but she just shook her head.

"You know, she hasn't even gotten up to shower?" She zipped up her lunch bag and made her way out the door.

Every time either of them removed the tray from Malkin's room, one or two items would be missing. Usually, it was a carton of milk, so she had to be consuming something, but he didn't know when.

On the third day, she got up and walked around her small box of a room. He looked in on her, but said nothing, just watched her. It was the middle of the night, not that she would necessarily know that considering the lack of a window. There was a clock just outside her door

for her to look at, but she never came to it.

She appeared to be content in her own timeless world.

She hummed a song he recognized, but couldn't quite pinpoint, and

floated about her quarters in her socks. Vincent watched her on the

surveillance camera in the orderly station. She looked like a sail in a

storm, cutting through each gust of wind with ease and grace. He found

himself humming along.

On the fourth night, after retrieving the dinner trays from the other

inmates' quarters, Vincent came upon Malkin's door. From habit, he

peeked in the room before bending down to grab the tray. For the first

time, he caught her eye.

His heart quickened as he looked away, fearing her stare. When he stood

back up, she had risen from her bed and was walking, almost gliding,

toward the door. His eyes were fastened to her as she moved. He was

entranced by the sway of her hips as she walked. Vincent couldn't help

but wonder if she purposely exaggerated her sway a little.

"Officer Kore, is it?" she asked.

"Yes, it is." He spoke firmly, though his insides were galloping.

"You've been watching rather intently the last few days, have you not?"
Her eyes didn't blink; they were glazed and heavy. Almost as if she were
intoxicated.

"No more than I check in on any other inmate here, Malkin," he
corrected.

"Prudence," she said, then turned away from him, returning to her bed.
Vincent stood there for a moment. His mind urgently told him to walk
away but he couldn't feel his legs to move them. She sat on her bed and
pulled up her legs to lie down, scooping her hair behind her ear. He
watched as she pulled her knees toward her chest and tucked her hands
between her thighs.

Regaining the feeling in his legs, Vincent quickly turned away and
proceeded to discard the dinner trays.

He avoided her cell for the rest of the night.

CHaPTer 6

The echoing of boots marching up and down the single narrow hall of solitary bounced off the walls and seeped into the cells as Officer Turner made her first rounds of the morning. Her red hair was wound up tight into a bun at the crown of her head. Strays wisped around her freckled, rosy cheeks. Her keys were hooked to her side on a belt loop and jingled fiercely as she went, calling into the cells at the inmates. If they didn't answer, she would unsheathe her baton and bang on their door to elicit a physical response. In anticipation of Officer Turner's arrival, Prudence sat up in her bed, pulling up and crossing her feet.

"Malkin!" Officer Turner chimed, peeking into her cell.

Prudence grimaced. "Officer Turner, I insist that you call me Prudence."

"Is that so?" she replied.

"No need for formalities, *just* Prudence."

Officer Turner waved for her to draw near, so she obliged.

"Alright, Prue. But you have to call me Gerty. I'm not big on formalities,

either." Her smile was so big, her cheeks almost buried her emerald

green eyes.

Sweet woman.

"Of course." Prudence nodded at Gerty and returned to her bed,

diverting her attention to Officer Kore, who had been on her mind

lately. She wasn't ignorant of the effect she had on him. Prudence could

feel him watching her in the night once Gerty left. Maybe it was because

he was concerned that she wasn't active, nor was she pleading for a

little recess like the rest.

She could hear them, pitiful, begging him to go for a walk or take a

second shower. Anything to leave the confines of these four pale, gray

walls. To her, the walls were a very tranquil shade; they made her feel at

ease.

And the silence.

Had she any belief in God, she would be certain he had created silence

especially for her. No one flirting with her, no loud and abrasive women,

nor the cackling fiends who surrounded the latter. No snoring in a bunk beneath her, no murmuring of those who gossiped around her. No *Officer* Benitez. Just placid silence.

Prudence was pleased that she chose to obtain her "get into solitary free" card by injuring that swine. It was like clockwork, him making his way to her at breakfast time to whisper something lascivious and vile into her ear. After she noticed the whispers stirring up unwanted feelings, she knew she had to remove herself wholly from his presence. Prudence was seated beside Berkeley that morning and was anxiously fidgeting with her fork under the table, scraping its prongs along the table's underbelly.

"Did you hear me?" asked Berkeley, her shrill voice sounding hurt by Prudence's perceived lack of interest in the conversation. Over the last couple of months, Prudence had grown fond of Berkeley. She served as an unexpected necessity that offered a distraction from all the unwanted and constant attention.

"Of course I heard you," she responded, throwing the fork back onto the tray of food she had neglected to touch.

"Say, Prue?" Berkeley adjusted in her seat. "You don't seem right. You feelin' ok?"

Prudence's eyes darted side to side. Her body was quaking ferociously, so much so that she couldn't shake the visible tremors she exhibited. She looked up at her acquaintance and forced a smile to hide her discomfort as best she could.

Berkeley's eyes traveled from Prudence to just past her, at Edgar approaching. She looked away almost bashfully, no doubt recounting the exchange she herself had with the oaf in order to obtain a carton of cigarettes. She confided in Prudence that she had since quit smoking. "I don't think I could go through that again," she had said.

Prudence turned to face him, though this time, upon seeing him, she felt a pull she had been dreading. Aside from a few fresh scrapes, the same smug smirk rested on his face; she knew he could tell she was starting to soften with each passing week. He was very aware of how her eyes began to smolder instead of holding their usual vacancy and he noticed how they drifted down to his crotch like a dog looking at a bone.

"How goes it today, Peaches?" Edgar asked, running his tongue over his teeth.

Prudence's heartbeat quickened and beads of sweat formed on the back of her neck. He was far too close, as he often was, and the stench of his cologne singed the hairs in her nose while simultaneously making her mouth water.

"Tell me, *Officer*," she said, her voice quivering. "What does a girl like me have to do to get a little...alone time around here?"

His chuckle was malicious as he put his hands on his knees and bent down in front of her. Leaning into her ear, he spoke low and heavy so that his breath lingered on her neck like fog on glass.

"Do you mean you're ready for seconds? Is your pussy *dripping* for me again?"

Prudence's eyes fluttered shut and she squirmed in her seat. He leaned back, looking down at her hands fastened between her thighs. Just as Edgar was about to speak again, she smiled and then headbutted him. She reached behind her, grabbed her food tray, and hit him across the face, then struck the back of his knees with it, causing him to collapse to the ground. The ringing in her ears was so loud, she didn't hear the sea of inmates shouting and roaring with laughter. It wasn't until she looked around that she noticed Berkeley had jumped across the table, away from the commotion, and that Edgar's fellow officers were charging toward her.

They grabbed her by the arms. Just as they started to pull her away from Edgar, who was rocking on the floor, cradling his face, she stomped down hard on his stomach and let out a loud cackle, her eyes wide and vicious. Prudence was starting to lose control of herself again. She had to figure out how to suppress these outbursts without succumbing to *him* again.

However, five days in and no alternative came to mind. Her desires were intensifying by the day and all she had were these gray walls. Though she loathed the idea of begging to leave the confines of her space, she had to expel some of the energy that was building up far too rapidly inside of her.

At the wake of day three, she started jogging around her room—a jog that quickly accelerated into a run that lasted for close to two hours. Still, she had more energy to burn. More intense sensations to deplete. She was growing restless like she had been before. Emotions that she felt only in times like this resurfaced. Prudence rose from her bed and peered at the clock on the white wall across from her room, listening to it tick, tick, tick. Each tick was a puncture in Gretchen. With this memory came tears for the poor woman for whom she hadn't expressed any remorse until now. Prudence cried ferociously, clutching the door of her cell as she slid to her knees. It frightened Gerty, who had not heard so much as a peep from Prudence in the past several days. She came by to console her, but Prudence just continued to cry.

"I'm fine," she assured her through her sobbing. "Let me be!"

The residual emotion of self-disdain entered her hardened heart, softening it like cold butter in a skillet. Then, finally, embarrassment burned her stomach, the flow of tears subsided, and she returned to her bed, filled with shame.

On night four, after her brief exchange with Officer Kore, Prudence immediately had to retire to her bed to touch herself. She imagined him standing there, watching her. She imagined how he would become hard at the sight of her and begin to stroke himself. She wanted him to come in and take her, though she knew he hadn't stayed.

Once she was through, Prudence was struck with an aggravation that she couldn't shake for the rest of the night. It was pathetic that the simple sight of a man sent her body into a frenzy. Nothing was helping, nothing was banishing these wretched sentiments from her mind. She needed this to stop.

I need my reality back.

"Hey, Prue. You wanna shower today or are you still happy in your personal brand of funk?" Gerty tapped on the door with her baton.

Must be 5:00 pm.

Gerty started her shower rounds at 3:00 pm, taking one inmate at a time to the single shower tucked in the back for solitary. Each inmate got 10 minutes, from what Prudence could tell.

"No, thank you. Maybe later," she replied. Gerty rolled her eyes.

"You've said that every time."

She walked away, back into the orderly station, and continued to play a game whose obnoxious music had begun to disturb Prudence to her core. Rolling her eyes, she looked down at the tray of cold food at her feet. She knelt and grabbed the carton of milk, then continued toward her bed. Between the bed and the wall, Prudence had pulled away her bed just enough for her to place the carton between the mattress and the wall, alongside four more cartons she had saved. The previous cartons had begun to expand from spoilage, she noticed.

Her stomach growled loudly. She knew she had to start eating; she just lacked the desire to do so. Returning to the tray, she took the bread roll and ate it, dipping it into the ice-cold, gravy-soaked, instant mashed potatoes between every bite. This would be enough to tide her over for now.

Prudence proceeded to pace the room, humming her song, trying to suppress her impulses a while longer. Blood was rushing through her veins nonetheless, and her fingertips felt like they were vibrating. She was feeling thoroughly overwrought, finding it hard to not break out into full-on convulsions. Though the humming helped to some extent, she knew she wouldn't be able to keep still for long.

The clock read 7:00 for the second time that day. Officer Kore should be strolling in soon. The door leading into the orderly station opened and closed twice. Prudence heard Gerty telling him that the dinner trays had already been retrieved and not to worry. He spoke softly to her so as not to reach the ears of the inmates and then proceeded to briefly look in on each of them, walking swiftly.

So swiftly that he nearly passed Prudence without a glance.

"Officer Kore!" she called out, sounding almost frantic. She cringed at her own desperation. He stopped abruptly and turned toward her door.

"Yes, Malkin?"

"May I please have a shower now?" she asked.

Officer Kore glanced behind him with a look of surprise, toward Gerty, who must not have left yet. Prudence sat up on her toes and peered around at Gerty as best she could. Gerty looked surprised too and shrugged before nodding "yes."

Prudence's heartbeat slowed slightly.

"Once I'm through with my rounds, you'll get your shower, Malkin," he said. A few groans of disapproval came from the other cells. "Quiet! Everyone is entitled to their daily shower and I don't want to hear shit about it!"

Prudence smirked, thinking maybe the cartons wouldn't be necessary after all. She backed away from her door, patiently waiting. The frantic vibrations that had completely overtaken her scarcely subsided.

"It's about goddamn time!" Gerty exclaimed, exiting solitary. Officer Kore spared another glance at Prudence's door, then walked off.

It wasn't long before he was back, unlocking the door to her cell for the first time since she had entered it. He walked in, towering over her, with a pair of handcuffs in one hand and a fresh clothing set and towel tucked under his opposite arm. He cuffed her wrists together and then led her out of the cell by the arm. She leaned into him slightly, feeling the warmth of his body against hers as they walked down the hall toward the shower room.

It was nothing like the shower room she was used to. There was no stall, no curtain, no mirror or sink. Just the showerhead jutting out of a tiled wall, a soap dispenser most likely filled with fragrance-free shower gel, a drain in the floor, and a hamper across from it to collect soiled laundry. Officer Kore rested the fresh linens on a stand by the door he shut behind them and then briefly uncuffed one of her wrists.

"Undress, please," he said, then faced away from her, though he was still able to view her in his peripherals in case she decided to revolt. His hands were fastened behind his back. Prudence smirked, pulling her shirt over her head.

"A gentleman to your core, Officer *Kore*." She pulled off her shoes, then her pants and panties in a single motion.

"Excuse me?" he asked, not looking at her.

"Just a little peculiar, don't you think?"

"What?"

"Well..." Prudence discarded her clothing in the hamper opposite the shower. "Upon our first, brief introduction, you saw me completely disrobed, yet now you insist on looking away as I undress."

"Standard policy, Malkin," he said plainly, though she could see the vein in his neck pulse viciously.

She desperately wanted to bite down on his neck.

"Prudence," she corrected. He finally glanced at her. "I have quite the enmity for my surname, you understand."

Without a word, Officer Kore cuffed her to a ring just below the showerhead and switched it on, handing her a washcloth. The water came out cold, causing Prudence's body to tense. Officer Kore's eyes fixed briefly on her breasts, whose peaks tightened instantly when they came in contact with the ice-cold water. The water warmed slowly, uncomfortably slow, causing her to shiver.

"Please, Officer, this water is far too cold," she pleaded. He walked toward her and felt the water himself.

"I'm sorry...Prudence. It just takes time. There's no temperature gauge on here." He was doing his best to not look directly at her. "If you move this way, you won't be directly under the water and can wait for it to warm up." He took her arm and moved her from beneath the water, her hand tugging uncomfortably against the handcuffs.

Prudence quivered beneath his modest touch.

"Maybe next time," she suggested, "you can start the shower before I undress."

"I apologize," he said, stepping away again. Vincent truly felt badly about how uncomfortable she was. This was his first time taking an inmate to shower room and he hadn't known it would take so long to warm up.

"Is there a reason I'm cuffed to the shower? Do inmates actually try to run?" Prudence waited for him to glance her way before crossing her arm over her breasts, hugging herself slightly so the tops of them swelled.

"Yes, you would be surprised what a desperate person would do," he replied, looking directly into her eyes as he spoke.

"Silly. Don't you think so?" she asked, testing the water with her foot, her eyes still fixed on his.

"Very."

"I'm sure you have stories, Officer Kore," she said, pumping soap into the cloth in the palm of her free hand and lathering it on her torso. Prudence felt a bit of excitement about getting clean. She had been resisting showers to concentrate on suppressing her impulses, though she should have learned her lesson by now.

She craved cleanliness.

"You have only five more minutes to shower, Prudence. I suggest you stop talking and finish up," he commanded, breaking their gaze.

She bathed in silence for a moment, submerging her head underneath the water, which was now borderline scorching. Gazing at him as she bathed, Prudence was taking him in completely. Officer Kore was quite the specimen, with alluring eyes and a stature purely meant to serve as a muse for Greek sculptors. She only wished she could get a better look at his hands, which he had fastened together behind his back.

"Officer Kore?"

"Prudence," he answered, still not turning to look at her.

"Could you help me, please? I can't quite reach my back to wash properly, if you don't mind?" Prudence gestured toward him with her washcloth.

Shaking his head and smirking in disbelief, Officer Kore replied, "We aren't playing these games today, Malkin."

"Prud—"

"Prudence! Prudence... It is a privilege to be allowed to shower this late in the first place, so don't push your luck, especially not with me," he threatened.

"You misunderstand me, Officer Kore. I have been without a shower for five days. I only wish to be thoroughly clean," she explained, but he was not swayed.

"And whose fault is that? You think I don't know what you're up to?" he asserted, unable to keep his eyes away from her. She could feel his eyes tracing her all over; he seemed to be as disheveled as she had been feeling lately.

His desperation was clear in his eyes now.

"I only wish to be clean," she persisted. "I mean no harm, nor do I want to cause you any discomfort. But, if it's all the same to you, I'd be greatly in your debt if you would assist me." Her eyes glazed over as she gazed up at him.

Officer Kore had come closer now, seeming to contemplate his next move. He had great empathy for her, she could tell. He hovered over her for a moment. She could smell his cologne now. Then he snatched the cloth from her hand.

"Turn around. Any funny business and shower time is over, understood?"

"Completely."

Prudence faced the wall and stood perfectly still like he asked, waiting to feel the cloth on her back. When she did, she let out a sigh of gratification. He washed her back so gently, almost carefully, like he was wiping the petals of a flower covered in dirt. It was so gentle, she found herself closing her eyes and leaning slightly into the running water. He was careful to steer clear of the top of her bottom, which she found rather charming, but things were moving much more slowly than she was accustomed to.

"Officer Kore?"

"Prudence."

"What is your first name?" she asked. He removed the towel from her back to indicate he was through and she turned to face him.

"Vincent."

He reached out to her to return the cloth, but instead of just retrieving it, she took a hold of his hand. His hands were large, the fingers long and thick. Heat rose in her cheeks as she looked back up at him. Prudence saw his eyes dart down to his hand in hers and then drift up to her breasts. Upon seeing this, she slowly attempted to rest his hand over her bare chest. His fingers twitched in anticipation as they neared her.

He swiftly tore away from her and shut off the water.

"Forgive me, Vincent," she said. He handed her a towel without looking

at her again. "I am, regrettably, only human."

CHaPTer 7

December 2018

Prudence's daily life had been ordinary or even less than. When it came to her job, she enjoyed working long hours at the office with few to no breaks. Immersing herself entirely in her work was invigorating for her as she enjoyed tedious detail oriented work. Crunching numbers, filing, problem solving, reporting and risk analysis assessments enabled her to remain as distant from people as possible. She didn't find joy or pleasure in what most people did, like eating or regular social interaction. Rather, she viewed them as unfortunate necessities. Her communications with people were brief and concise so as not to take time away from her work.

In her personal life, Prudence had no desire to keep a boyfriend. The constant interaction with another individual was profoundly daunting to her. Nor did she care to meet the needs of another.

Handling her own needs was a feat of its own.

She was completely happy in her world alone, which made it all the more baffling to her when she found herself needing interactions, mostly sexual, with another when her impulses reached the peak of their intensity.

Prudence had been stifling a similar impulse for days when she received a phone call from Gretchen about her rent being overdue. She was never late on rent, but she was so thoroughly entrapped in her own downward spiral that she couldn't bring herself to act rationally.

She had to try to cure the inclination the usual way and get back on track.

Prudence sat at her desk at work. Her skin was crawling. Sweat beaded up on her upper lip and her heart pounded. Neglecting her duties, she impatiently stared at the black screen of her cell phone, waiting for it to illuminate with a notification that she was anticipating.

After what felt like forever in her restless mind, her phone pinged and a

banner with the name "Edgar" popped up on top of her screen.

Prudence had found him on a dating app, the kind you go to for a

quickie. They had been texting all morning. Considering how frank he

was about his intentions, coupled with the convenience of him also

being fairly attractive, she decided he would have to do.

                              3:27 pm

Edgar: How long before you're off?
Edgar: I need to take a bite of that peach.
Prudence: I need you.
Edgar: ;)
Prudence: I need you right now.
Prudence: Send me your address and I'll leave.
Edgar: 439 Congress St.
Prudence: Omw be ready.

She immediately plugged his address into google maps to find that his

apartment was only three blocks away. Prudence logged out of her

computer, threw on her coat, shoved her phone into her purse and

headed for the door.

"Prue?" her boss Mrs. Rizzo wheeled her chair out of her office when she noticed her running past. Prudence stopped so abruptly she almost tripped before turning back around.

"Where are you headed? It's not quite 4."

Prudence took a deep jagged breath and in that moment she decided she would have to run to Edgar's apartment instead of taking her car. She had a disturbing inkling that she'd need the extra exertion to nullify this particular impulse.

Thank god I wore my boots today.

"I'm, uh, I'm sorry Mrs. Rizzo, I failed to mention I have an appointment this afternoon. I have to go."

"Oh, I hope everything is alright." Mrs. Rizzo's wrinkled lips pursed as she looked Prudence up and down. "Please don't forget to notify me in advance next time Prue, you're usually much better about these things."

"Of course, have a good evening."

With that Prudence was out the door, purse clenched under her arm. The air was freezing cold, pinching her cheeks, moisture on her eyelashes crystallizing in the wind. Snow started to fall, the ground beneath her feet was becoming slick, but that didn't slow her pace as she ran.

She was desperate, panicked even.

When she arrived, her skin beneath the heavy wool coat was moist from sweat and her hair was disheveled, but that only seemed to make Edgar want her more. He licked the salty substance from her neck before biting down hard, pulling her coat off of her. Her body surged abruptly as his teeth sank deeper. Grabbing her by the waist, Edgar carried Prudence inside, kissing her as he did. She held firmly onto his biceps, growing more lascivious by the second. He threw her down, hiked her bottom into the air, pushed up her skirt and pulled down her tights. "Goddamn!" Edgar exclaimed, slapping her bottom as hard as he could. Prudence shrieked, her face was flat on the cold, tiled floor, her hot breath creating a moist fog over it. Undoing his own pants, Edgar removed his manhood, licked his hand, and smacked her sex over her panties, which were soaked through the fabric. Prudence was shaking vigorously as he slid her panties to the side and entered her, reaching around to grope her breasts. He took her there on the floor in front of the door, hard and furiously.

Even after they finished, and after she ran back to the parking garage just beside her office building, Prudence still felt unsettled. She needed more, somehow. She was fearful of what she would do, what she so desperately *needed* to do.

Only after the fact did Prudence realize that she should have answered the phone when Gretchen called the day before. If she had, Gretchen wouldn't have felt obliged to visit her that particular evening.

She would most assuredly still be alive had Prudence just answered the fucking phone.

CHAPTER 8

"Only human," she said.

Vulnerable and *human* was what he had been feeling far too often when in the same vicinity as her. Instinctively human, wanting to grab her by the waist and whisk her away. He felt so human that he was mortified at the thought of her having to be in a place like this; locked up behind bars. Vincent's growing compassion for her was unmatched and the bold way she expressed interest in him was frightening. He was too aware of her and too aware of his feelings for her. This was why he had moved to solitary in the first place, after all. He knew that resisting her was hardly an option.

Vincent sat on his bed, his feet in untied boots, gazing at the mirror across from him. His hair was a tousled mess, his shirt only partially buttoned. Dark circles deepened the appearance of his eyes. He was immobilized, unsure how to conduct himself at work that evening. He'd scolded her and warned her that she wouldn't be permitted to shower after hours again.

But he was not confident he could uphold this rule.

The clock read 7:10 pm when he strolled into the orderly's station to relieve Gerty. Her hands were propped on her tummy and she leaned back in her chair, watching a show on her phone.

"Oh! Seven already?" she said, turning in the swivel chair to face him, not noticing he was late.

"Slow day?" he asked, retrieving his clipboard.

"The girls have been pretty good today. Oh, and Collins is back."

"Collins? Why?" he asked, leaning against the counter.

"Ah, girl just knows how to rack up those shots. They're talking about moving her to a higher security facility since coming here every few months doesn't seem to be doing the trick." Gerty gathered her things and headed for the door. "On a lighter note, Malkin took another shower

today. She worked up quite a sweat running around in her cell."

"Oh...well, that's good," Vincent replied, vague disappointment in his

tone. Gerty must not have caught it because she was out the door

without another word.

Vincent lingered in the office for well over an hour before making his

rounds, wery of getting close to her again. Eventually he continued out

of the station and checked in on the inmates, most of whom—including

Prudence—were now asleep. He was relieved that he didn't have to see

her gazing at him right away; he couldn't be sure that he wouldn't burst

in and take her there on the floor of her cell. He felt so ashamed for

where his mind was taking him, like he was under her enticing spell.

Was she a siren? A temptress sent to lure him to a merciless death with

her song?

He made his way back to the orderly's station and sat in the swivel chair,

which was still warm from Gerty's behind. He filled out several

behavioral forms for the inmates who were reaching the end of their

stay in solitary, then filed a few things that Gerty had left scattered

across the countertop. Next, he spent some time fidgeting with a pen

before he started to drift off to sleep.

A few minutes later, after jolting awake, Vincent decided he should review the surveillance cameras in the inmate's cells as a means to check on them while keeping his distance. He'd had trouble resting when he got home from work early that morning and he hoped doing this would keep him from drifting again for at least a little while.

As he clicked through each cell, sleeping inmate after sleeping inmate appeared on the screen until he ultimately came upon Prudence. She was up, pacing her cell, glancing at the door from time to time. She seemed restless, agitated even.

Is she looking for me?

Vincent propped his chin on his hands and watched her pace. Prudence stopped abruptly and stared at her bed for a moment, then put her hands on the frame and smashed it suddenly into the wall repeatedly. Vincent jumped up and ran out towards her cell.

"Prudence?" he called out once he reached her door, a putrid smell reaching his nose. "Prudence, what are you doing?" She looked up at him, relieved to see he came so quickly. She knew he'd be watching.

"I seemed to have made a mess, Officer Kore," she remarked, gesturing at the puddle of curdled milk coming from under her bed and the splatter it made on her clothes.

Frustration bubbled up within him as Vincent opened her cell. "Hands on the wall!"

She paused a moment, then turned to face the wall, putting both hands on it as he had requested. Vincent came up behind her and took down her hands one by one, cuffing them.

"Now sit over there where I can see you."

Again, she obliged. He left the cell, locking her back in for a moment, and retrieved the cleaning supplies from the closet beside the orderly station. First, he stripped the bed and discarded the bedding in a laundry sack. From her seat on the floor, Prudence silently watched him clean. He seemed to be angry with her, which she could understand, but this was necessary.

A cry for help, if you will.

He left again, then returned with a single blanket and pillow, which he threw on the bed.

"Am I not to have a shower, Officer Kore?" she asked when he went to unshackle her wrists.

"Why are you doing this?" he asked, jerking her around to face him. Her clothes reeked of spoiled milk.

"A change of clothes at the very least?" she asked, her glazed eyes

peering into his so deeply that he grew even more anxious than he'd

been before. He grabbed her by the collar and pulled her to him. "I

should leave you in them as punishment."

Prudence sharply inhaled the scent of his breath, staring at his bare

teeth. There was a different, more effective, punishment she had in

mind.

"But you won't," she whispered, "will you, Vincent?"

He shoved her away from him, irritated as he rubbed the back of his

neck.

She was right. He wouldn't.

"You won't get this privilege again, got it?"

Vincent escorted her out of the cell and down to the shower room. He

could hardly believe what he was doing, couldn't believe the

vulnerability he was allowing her to witness. He felt shame burn his

cheeks, but he couldn't stop himself from allowing his pent-up

emotions to seep out.

He pulled her into the shower room and shut the door. Then he started

the shower, allowing time to warm.

"What were you doing with all those milk cartons in there? Huh? What's the matter with you?" he asked her.

Prudence didn't answer, just stood there with a small smile on her face. Vincent walked past her to test the water, then uncuffed one of her hands so she could undress. He turned away as she did.

She laughed under her breath. "You have my permission to look, Vincent."

"I think I'll stick with procedure," he snapped, then cuffed her to the wall. "Take your shower quickly."

Prudence tried to do as he asked. She stepped underneath the running water and pumped soap into the palm of her hand. He hadn't provided a washcloth this time. Judging by his demeanor she knew he wanted her, but perhaps he was too angry for her to push too aggressively. In spite of every atom of her being erupting simultaneously, she pushed herself to be more deliberate.

Urgent, but deliberate.

She lathered her body with soap, leisurely caressing her breasts, running her fingers over and down her stomach to just above her sex. Her eyes burned into him, lids hung heavy, lips parted. But Vincent was seemingly immovable.

Seemingly.

Prudence lathered more soap between her palms and reached her back as best she could, but like before, was having trouble washing it thoroughly.

"Officer Kore?" she began. He peered at her finally from the corner of his eye. "I won't ask you to wash me again. I understand I crossed a line with that. But if you could just switch the cuff to my opposite wrist, I'll be able to manage on my own."

He walked over to her, looking down on her as he did. "You ask for a lot, Prudence."

"Forgive me," she said. He had gotten so close now that her wet breasts pressed up against him.

He couldn't stop himself.

His wall of restraint came tumbling down as he moved her to the side and pushed her up against the wall. Water dampened his sleeve.

"Seeing as I just had to clean up your filthy mess after having already done you a favor, I'd say you owe me. And I intend to get what I'm owed." He looked her up and down, no longer adhering to modesty. He couldn't help it, though a voice screamed in his head for him to back off.

"Do you want me...Vincent?" Prudence bit down on her lip to suppress a smile.

She knew the answer.

She brought her leg up along his side to anchor him to her. Vincent's hand traced from the top of her thigh down to the bend in her knee, pulling it up slightly as he knelt to the ground before her. Even on his knees, his eyes were level with her chest. He lifted her leg over his shoulder and brought the other leg up as well, the handcuff pulling at her wrist as she was lifted, before burying his face between her thighs. First, she felt the tickle of his beard against her. The dew of her awakened sex dripped down her thighs and under her bottom. She almost climaxed instantaneously the moment his tongue met her clit. She quivered so violently, she feared she would fall, but he kept her still. He ate away at her like he had been starved for weeks, drinking her in completely until nothing was left and then still persisted. Her fingers tangled in his hair, tugging when it was almost too much to bear. Water from the still-running shower trickled in his hair and over his back. Vincent's fingers dug into her so tightly, bruises began to form. Prudence wrapped her legs firmly around his neck as she came a second time.

He removed her from his shoulders, her moisture dripping from his beard. She leaned against the wall to keep herself up, legs buckling as her sex continued to pulsate. She watched him unbutton his uniform, watched as his broad chest emerged from beneath it. Her body quickened once more. She gazed at him as he pulled his cock from his briefs. It throbbed in his hands as he caressed it, closing the space between them and looking down at her again.

He took her face in his hand and kissed her with so much force, she fell into him, grasping his arm for support, their tongues dancing. As they kissed, he reached down and slid a finger inside her, then two. All the while, his thumb rubbed against her clit. Her moans vibrated against his open mouth. Prudence's sex squeezed tight around his fingers and she dug her nails into his arm as he continued to bring her body to its very limits.

Vincent intended to take her as he wanted, to have her endure every last ounce of the pent-up tension he had been suppressing. With his other hand, he caressed her throat before tightening his grip around it, pulling away from their kiss. He watched her lips pout and her eyes roll back in her head as she relinquished complete control.

"Touch me," he ordered, so she did, reaching down and taking his girth in her hand. She stroked him tenaciously, letting out a muffled shriek as he slipped in a third finger. Vincent squeezed her throat tighter to prevent any more sound from escaping, then drilled into her wildly.

Prudence came, shuddering again as she did, but he wasn't through. He

spun her around and pushed her against the wall, pulling her uncuffed

wrist behind her back, forcing her to take every last inch of him. She

cried out. Just as she did, he grabbed her throat from behind, quickening

his pace feverishly. Vincent gawked at her bottom, watching it rebound

against his pelvis, water cascading down both of their bodies. He

slapped it hard on one side, then the other. She shuddered each time he

did it, tightening up around his cock.

"Is this what you've wanted, Prue? Huh?" Vincent growled in her ear.

"You wanted me to break. You wanted me to give in." He smacked her

harder and she cried out, "Yes!"

He clamped his hand over her mouth, pulled up one of her legs, and

pounded into her harder. He urged her to take it, holding her in place

until he was through. He felt her cum again and again on his cock,

fueling him to penetrate deeper until he felt his own climax coming

rapidly. He pulled out of her and came all over her sore, red bottom and

back.

Vincent led Prudence back to her cell, fresh and clean. Once the door was locked, he looked in on her to find that she had already laid down to sleep. He had felt regret the moment they finished, but now he felt even worse.

She said nothing when he was through.

Didn't look at him as the two of them dressed. Her eyes were no longer glazed. The heat in her cheeks had simmered. She seemed to have detached herself from their shared moment.

Had he violated her?

Was she disappointed in him?

He was sure he had correctly read all the signs she was giving, but maybe he had been wrong. A knot forming in the pit of his stomach, Vincent made his way back to the orderly's station, briefly peeking in on the other inmates, afraid one of them may have heard them. He looked in on Collins, who sat awake on her bed. She looked back at him, laughing. "Didn't see that coming from you, Kore."

"Excuse me, Collins?" he erupted, nervously tugging at his saturated collar.

She threw up her hands. "Hey, I don't know nothin'. Just hope the
year's worth of jizz didn't kill whoever you just fucked." Her eyebrow
shot up, leaning forward in her bed, "Was it Prudence?"

His cheeks flushed.

"Yeah, I bet it was. I have to say, I'm a little jelly."

"Fuck off, Collins, or I'll increase your cell time to 23 and a half hours. Is
that understood?" he barked.

She lifted her hands again and proceeded to lay down. He walked away,
glaring at her viciously, then ran his hands through his damp hair.

His clothes were damp as well, and his beard smelled profoundly of her
essence, which continued to intoxicate him. A million thoughts about
Prudence ran through Vincent's mind, even more now that he had
finally taken her.

Come 3:00 am, Vincent made his last rounds to check on the inmates
before his shift ended. He figured Prudence would still be asleep when
he made his way to her cell, but he couldn't resist looking in on her
before he left. He wanted so badly to talk to her, to make sure he didn't
overstep a boundary. He wanted her to know that this was not what he
was usually like.

Vincent replayed their encounter in his mind a hundred times more on his drive home and in his bed well into the night, staring at the ceiling. Even Brocc's noisy snoring couldn't disrupt his train of thought. It wasn't until the sun rose and its rays pierced the blinds of his window that Vincent finally drifted off to sleep.

"Buddy?" said Gallagher, who was now knocking on Vincent's locker to get his attention. "Buddy, you alright? I've been talking to you for about five minutes now and you ain't said a word yet."

Vincent shut the locker door, shaking the sleep from his head. "I'm sorry. I couldn't sleep for shit last night."

"What, Broccoli being a menace?" Gallagher asked, tightening his laces.

"No, never." Vincent took a seat on the bench in the middle of the locker room, rubbing his eyes again, making them more red and irritated.

"Then what's up?" Gallagher asked, sitting beside him.

Vincent looked around, watching the last of the officers make their way out of the locker room. Then he walked over to the door and locked it. When he turned to walk back toward his friend, Gallagher's face was etched with concern. His mustache twitched into an unsure smile.

"That serious, huh?"

"Pretty fucking serious, man," he replied sitting back down across from Gallagher. "You remember how Pru—Malkin made her way into solitary?"

"Ha. Shit, yeah. Heard Edgar should be back in a day or two. Big-ass crybaby," he scoffed, shaking his head.

"Well, she was really quiet the first few days. Didn't eat, didn't sleep. Then one day she starts talking to me."

Gallagher shifted.

"And she's kind of...flirtatious with me."

"Ah, that's not unheard of, Vin. All of those chicks do that down there."

"No, I know. Believe me. But Malkin...I don't know how to explain it."

Vincent scratched the back of his neck, losing track of what he meant to say, wondering why he was bothering to confess anything at all.

"Did something happen with you two?" Gallagher asked after a moment.

Vincent's eyes avoided him. Every ounce of amusement drained from his face. "Really, Vin? You can't be serious right now."

"I know, I know." Vincent's head fell. He could feel the disappointment in Gallagher's gaze. "Prudence is just...I don't know, different? A—and anyway, right after, she just went blank."

"Blank?" The concern in Gallagher's brow deepened.

"Yeah, like nothing happened. Didn't say anything, just went straight to bed. Didn't even look at me."

Gallagher shifted again in his seat on the bench and came face to face with Vincent. "Look, you're my best friend and I love you. But that just sounds like an inmate who needed some dick. I'm sorry if that's not what you want to hear, but that's what I'm picking up here."

"I don't think it's that simple, Joe. I think there's more to her," Vincent said, feeling stupid the moment he did.

"I hear you and I know you've got a tender heart, but I'm telling you, don't get in deep shit over an inmate. Be careful."

Vincent tried to heed his friend's advice. Maybe she did just need to get laid. But something about it wasn't right. The way she went about it was unlike anything he had ever come across. It was much more calculated than any other inmate, who would have had the gumption to just come right out with their intentions and grab his cock. The way Prudence

looked at him, the way she seduced him.

He had to know that he hadn't made a mistake.

CHaPTer 9

N ow day six, Prudence woke without an ounce of dread or urgency.

She was no longer bogged down by the intense overflow of emotion that
brought up thoughts, fears and sensations she would never usually be
concerned with.

Prudence finally cracked open the book she had acquired from the cart
that Gerty had brought around in the first few days. Gerty had been
barking at Prudence to return the book so that someone else could have
a turn, but she simply couldn't focus on anything at the time. Prudence
sat quietly for the entire day, her thoughts engulfed by the story she
read. She neglected to eat even her roll. The dinner tray lacked a milk

carton, she noticed, which was mildly humorous. Officer Kore must have told Gerty about the *milk incident* the night before.

Prudence was also notified that her time in solitary had been increased. This she didn't particularly mind. Now that she felt better, it would be time well spent.

Thinking of the night before, Prudence couldn't help but feel thankful to Officer Kore for his help, as she would call it. Aside from this, she had felt perfectly normal immediately after they finished and slept more soundly than she had in days.

She was finishing a chapter in her book when she heard the clanging shudder of the slot at the bottom of her door. Completing the last few words in the sentence that she had started, Prudence looked up over the top of the book and glanced down at the floor to see what had been delivered.

It was a piece of folded paper.

She dog-eared the page to hold her place and set the book on the bed beside her before gingerly walking over to the note. She picked it up and looked briefly out the window in her door to see if the messenger had lingered. There stood Officer Kore. He wasn't looking in on her, just standing, waiting.

The note read:

Prudence,

   I wanted to ask if you were ok.

When she looked up from the note, he remained looking away until she

tapped on the window with her fingernails. He looked in. Once he did,

she mimed a pen on paper, to which he responded by sliding them

through the slot.

He was prepared.

Fine.

He read the note, paused, then scribed a new one.

Are you sure? I didn't take advantage of you, did I?

She read it, then looked up at him. Worry lingered heavily in his eyes.

"You're overthinking this, trust me," she said, then returned to her book.

Just as she sat down and turned to the page she had marked, the slot clanged again.

Another note.

If I did something out of line, please speak up.

Prudence sighed, ripped the note off the pad, and started a new one.

You assisted me greatly. I thank you. Good night.

Vincent looked up at her from the note, at which point she shooed him away with a flick of her hand, then returned to her book. When she didn't hear the slot clang again, she assumed he had walked away. But he lingered a moment, thoroughly perplexed. She was treating it as if they'd had some sort of business transaction. Like he was a porno flick she had rented from the local 24-hour adult video store and that she was ready to return.

Vincent couldn't wrap his mind around it.

He scratched the back of his neck as he walked back into the orderly station, the sound of snoring inmates coming from various cells. He was beginning to feel the way he feared he had made her feel.

Used, violated.

His heart was toyed with, had to have been, because she could clearly see how she affected him. How he couldn't resist obliging her every need, including one he found to be so indecent. Vincent wanted to feel angry, to lash out by removing her book privileges or something, but he simply couldn't. He felt he was in the wrong for falling for it just as much as she was for initiating it.

◆

"Phil, you think this thing has enough head on it?" Vincent said, watching the foam trickling over the lip of his mug, knowing that Phil's retort would be swift.

"I've never heard of anyone complaining about getting too much head." He winked, then bellowed an infectious guffaw. He strolled down the bar to incoming guests. Gallagher already had his IPA in front of him, half-empty.

"So, you talked to her, huh?" he asked, popping another fried cheese curd into his mouth before wiping the grease from his fingers onto his uniform pants.

"Not exactly," Vincent said. He handed his friend a napkin and took a long, hard gulp of his beer, wiping the foam from his mustache. "I slipped notes into her cell."

Gallagher choked on a curd and laughed. "Notes? Vin, come on."

"I didn't want to talk out loud for others to hear," he snapped, shifting in his seat and redirecting his eyes to the television.

"Got it, ok. Well?"

"Well. She just said I helped her out and *thanked* me. Then she told me I'm overthinking it."

Gallagher scoffed, sliding his empty pint away from him, Phil glided over and retrieved a chilled pint glass from a cooler in front of the seated officers, then proceeded to fill it with Gallagher's preferred beer of the night.

"Told ya. She just wanted to fuck. You can't get attached to this woman, Vin. You're too sensitive," Gallagher said, pulling his fresh pint to him and taking a small sip. "And even if she was actually interested, it's not like she'll get to come home with you, meet your ma, cuddle your dog at

night while you watch *Parks and Rec.*"

"You're right, I know you're right..." Vincent shook his head and looked

away from Gallagher, his brain muddled. "But it's like I'm Mercury and

she's the fucking sun."

"You've got to let her go."

Vincent slumped slightly in his seat, downing the last half of his stout.

He didn't want to let her go, not just yet. He needed to understand,

needed to know what was going on in Prudence Malkin's mind.

Or, at the very least, he had to try.

Vincent rolled his near-empty mug back and forth in his hand, the glob

of foam sliding down. Its size was laughable compared to that of his

hands.

The door creaked open and in walked Edgar, who quickly took a seat next

to Gallagher once he spotted them settled at the bar. Vincent glared at

him, noticing the yellowed bruises on his cheek and forehead, coupled

with his own handiwork, which was almost completely healed. He

clenched his fists under the bar, his knuckles popping.

"Hey, faggots. How's it been?" Edgar blurted out, "Hey! A Bud!"

"Benitez, you don't have to yell at the guy. He'll get here when he gets here," Gallagher stated, scooping up another handful of curds.

"Fuck that guy, it's his job. Hey, Kore, no hard feelings!" Edgar called out across Gallagher. Vincent sighed deeply before retrieving his fresh pint from Phil. "How's Malkin doing in solitary, huh?"

Vincent didn't reply. Phil threw a pint of beer haphazardly in front of Edgar.

"What a fucking cunt, right?"

Vincent paused for a beat, the lip of the mug barely brushing his mustache.

He was asking for trouble today.

"Why, because she took your bitch ass out?" Gallagher quipped, laughing uproariously at his own joke. Vincent took his sip.

Edgar popped him on the back. "Come on, man. She caught me off guard. You both know I would have had that bitch on the ground, two seconds flat." Both Gallagher and Vincent scoffed audibly. "You fucks just don't know the whole story."

"What else is there? You pushed the wrong buttons with the wrong one this time, Benitez." Gallagher told him, shaking his head. He peeked over at Vincent, who sat perfectly still, his jaw tensing.

"No, I mean the *whole* story. Before Malkin got locked up." Edgar was leaning in close to them, eager to air out his dirty laundry, as always. This made Vincent uneasy, anxious about what Edgar was hankering to dredge up.

The history of Prudence?

A mild explanation, perhaps?

He shuddered at the idea of her having a history of any sort, no matter how miniscule, with this arrogant louse, but he needed to know.

"I fucked her." Edgar's words oozed out like sewage from a drainage pipe, making Vincent's stomach flip and curdle. "She was all over me, begging for it. Who am I to deny a fine girl like that? Me and her had been texting. She found me online somewhere, had only started that day and she was—ooh—she was ready. Asked to meet up at my place. So I gave her my info and not an hour later she was there."

"You can't be fucking serious," Gallagher exclaimed, beguiled by Edgar's retelling.

"Oh, I'm serious. When am I not serious?" Edgar swigged at his pint and set it back down, a smug grin on his face when he looked over at Vincent, who had grown visibly uncomfortable. "Yeah, she came over and barely got in the door before we were fucking on my floor. It was hot." He started to laugh as he reminisced.

Vincent put his mug on the bar top, worried he'd launch it at Edgar's face.

"Something wrong, Vin? You jealous?"

"I don't believe a fucking word you say. Shut the fuck up and drink that piss you call beer," Vincent asserted. His rage was building and he knew he had to leave. "Phil, can I have my tab, please?"

Phil nodded and went straight for the register to grab his ticket.

Edgar leaned back in his stool, taking another sip. "Why would I lie, huh?"

"Oh, I don't know. Maybe because your overinflated ego has been shot," Vincent replied, trying to convince himself.

"No, no, no. It happened and that girl's got a problem. A big nympho problem," Edgar went on. Vincent's face was heating up. Gallagher tried to interject, but Edgar proceeded. "That night after she left my place, she fucking killed a lady. There's something wrong with her, big time. But hey, I'd hit it again if I got the chance." Edgar's grin widened at how uncomfortable Vincent had become, "That pussy was too good."

Vincent shot up from his stool, nearly knocking it over. Gallagher

jumped up in response to stand between them. "Alright, alright."

Edgar rose. "You wanna say something, Kore? You got a sweet spot for

the crazy nympho in solitary?"

Vincent's fists clenched, whitening his knuckles and causing the veins

in his forearm to pulsate. The patrons near them in the pub started to

take notice of the brewing commotion and grew silent. Phil was already

making his way over.

"Guys, you need to take it outside," he said, pushing Vincent's tab

toward him.

Vincent continued to snarl, "Fuck you, Edgar, you disgusting pig."

He threw down a wad of cash and headed for the door. Edgar started to

laugh and Gallagher called out for Vincent, but he didn't stop. Fury

seeped into every crevice of his body as he made his way to his car and

jumped inside. Though he didn't want to believe the bile that Edgar was

regurgitating, he felt like the man was telling the truth.

He was nauseous just thinking about Prudence having slept with him.

Him of all people.

What would possess her to do such things?

Vincent remembered reading her case file a few weeks after she came to the prison. He'd been curious as to why someone with her composure ended up in such a place. He'd read all the public records on her case, but there was no mention of a reason or motive for her reckless behavior; just her confession and full cooperation.

Her confession was so concise, you would assume she was reading straight from a medical examiner's report, down to the size of the knife she used. It was unfathomable.

If Edgar's crude story did anything at all, it made Vincent crave more information about who she had been prior to her incarceration. As of now, it would seem she was dangerously impulsive.

Perhaps she was exactly where she belonged.

CHAPTER 10

Showers with Gerty, Prudence came to find, were painstakingly

annoying. All the woman did was talk, despite Prudence's

understanding that solitary confinement was meant to be rather silent

and restrictive. But this poor woman, with an ability to ramble and carry

on entire discussions on her own, wouldn't resist engaging in repartee

any chance she got. Though it was mildly understandable, the woman's

phone was used purely for garbage television and mindless games. Pair

all that with her being an officer stationed in solitary confinement and it

was apparent why she would have such a sensational appetite for

conversation.

Unfortunately, she was barking up the wrong tree with Prudence.

"Now, I'm not saying I agree with the way Jerry coaxes some of his guests, but you've got to admit, it makes for great TV!" Gerty droned on, looking down at her phone as Prudence bathed.

"I don't bother with television," Prudence stated, rinsing the suds from her hair.

Gerty's eyebrows shot up. "Like zero TV?"

Prudence shook her head in response.

"What do you do for fun?"

"Puzzles, books. Television isn't all there is, Gerty."

"Did you have a monthly book club or something with your friends?" Gerty asked, lowering the volume on her device. She wasn't accustomed to Prudence contributing so much to their talks.

"No friends. Didn't need them."

"Who doesn't need friends? I only have, like, two really good friends, but I think I'd die without them. You must have had a solid boyfriend to keep you happy without friends," she said. Her phone found its way into her pocket.

"No boyfriend. Just me, my books, and my puzzles," she replied. Prudence bathed her back to the best of her ability, still unable to reach it properly due to one wrist being cuffed, which irked her.

"Cat? Dog?"

This initiated a glare from Prudence.

"Is it true that Collins is in solitary at this time?" Prudence asked, putting a stop to her prying. Gerty was clearly puzzled. Prudence could see a visible shift in her train of thought as she racked her brain for an answer.

One aspect of their conversations that surprisingly piqued her interest was Gerty's gossip about the other inmates in solitary. She told her about the crimes that had landed them in prison. A pair of women were there for murdering their children, another for accepting money from a man in exchange for sex with her son.

Neglect, sexual assault.

The list went on.

To hear about how these women mistreated their children made Prudence's blood boil in a way she was not accustomed to feeling. Especially not when she was in her 'calm state.'

"Uh, yeah. How do you know that?" Gerty asked.

"I was sure I heard her voice. Did she pimp her children out for drugs, too?" Prudence asked, fully expecting her story to be just as deplorable.

"No, no. Collins killed a guy," Gerty replied. "Her cousin, I think. She found out he had been raping her daughter." Prudence's stomach sank and the hairs on her arms stood up. It was shocking that such a hardened woman like Collins had the capacity to love and protect someone else. Even more surprising that she had a daughter. An unfamiliar warmth enveloped Prudence's heart in response to Collins' regard for her child.

Gerty looked down at her phone to check the time. "Alright, Prue, you have overstayed your welcome. Wrap it up!"

Prudence shook her head, knowing the only reason her showers lasted so long was because of Gerty's insatiable need to run her mouth. But it was neither here nor there. She dried off and got dressed before being led back to her cell.

Prudence took some time to ponder the idea of Collins and who she was. It was something she hadn't bothered or found reason to even consider doing. Collins' company had been unbearable, to say the least. Even after their first meeting, she kept coming back to antagonize and flirt with Prudence. It was almost every day, on top of having to listen to Edgar relay his fantasies every morning at the crack of dawn.

Prudence and Collins received a few shots between the two of them based on their encounters. She was never one to be easily coerced into even a minor disagreement. Minute things of the like never fazed her, but being in this place was doing something to her state of mind she didn't like. Collins wouldn't stop encouraging her to unmask primitive feelings and irrational behavior.

It was proving to be too much.

Though, now that she was thinking about the matter of her brutish companion, she felt pity.

She was a woman convicted of a just crime, in Prudence's opinion, unable to raise and continue to protect her child. In a way, she understood Collins' aggression and need to lash out. She never would have thought Collins to be so decent and courageous.

Clang.

Prudence, who was resting on her bed, rolled over to face the cell door. On the floor, she saw a note. She sighed, not bothering to look up to see if Officer Kore stood there, then rolled back over to face the wall again. There was a reason she never contacted the same man in the past; she didn't want them to grow attached. It would seem, however, that this was not something she could easily avoid here.

Vincent stood there a moment, but when he saw her roll over, he knew she wasn't going to be bothered with his notes. He continued with his rounds and made his way back into the orderly station, where he set the monitor on Prudence's cell to see when she would pick up the note. If she would pick up the note. She never did. The following day, when he came in for his shift, Edgar was in the locker room, spreading the news about his apparent affair with Prudence, though this retelling was much more elaborate, with details about Prudence's naked body and the sounds she made as she moaned, "Loud enough for the neighbors to hear! I literally got calls from the leasing office telling me I had multiple complaints!" Everyone laughed. Gallagher walked over to Vincent, who stood at his locker. It was no surprise that someone as deplorable as Edgar would need to tarnish and discredit the name of anyone who made an example of him, especially when that person was a woman. "Hey, man, you alright? I haven't talked to you since the other night," he inquired.

"I'm good," Vincent replied, closing his locker door. "Thanks."

Edgar continued once the laughter had died down. "I mean, this bitch was wet when she got there and all she had seen was my profile picture. Just dripping!" Vincent wanted so badly to not hear him, but all he could do was quickly finish and get out of there as soon as he could.

"Hey, Vin! Where you running off to?" Edgar baited. Out of the corner of his eye, he had caught Vincent trying to depart.

"Gotta start my shift, Benitez," he replied.

"Don't you want to hear the rest of the story? I'm sharing some juicy details over here. Oh wait, but you've already seen her naked, haven't you?"

Vincent froze. "What?"

"I mean, you were in the ladies shower room her first day." Edgar walked through the gathering of men and toward Vincent. "You saw, right?" Edgar searched his eyes, waiting for a reply, knowing he was tickling a nerve with the big guy.

"I went in to defuse an altercation, not to ogle at the inmates. That's more like something you'd pull."

Edgar smiled wide. The nerve was even more sensitive than he'd previously thought. He leaned in and whispered in Vincent's ear. "You like her, huh? How long has she been in solitary with you?"

Vincent's nostrils flared. His heartbeat quickened and his fists

clenched. "Fuck. Off." Hushed conversations erupted throughout the

locker room, Vincent's anger shifted to worry.

"Lay off, Benitez. Everyone knows Vin would never touch an inmate."

Gallagher stepped in, patting Vincent on the back and leading him away.

Once they were out of earshot, Gallagher said, "Don't worry about them

telling the warden anything. They have no proof for one and two, we

have so much dirt on Benitez, he'd be a moron to try anything."

"I'm so close to beating him within an inch of his life. That fuck makes

my skin crawl."

Vincent didn't bother trying to communicate with her that day. He just

marked her off on his clipboard and carried on down the row. He

collected their dinner trays and disposed of them promptly before

making his way back to the orderly station, where he sat for the last

couple hours, clicking through the various surveillance cameras.

Each time he came across Prudence's cell, she was reading, whereas

most of the inmates had already gone to sleep. The third go-round,

Vincent lingered on her for a while. She wagged her foot off the edge of

the bed, running through the pages of her book like rapids down a creek. He imagined this was similar to how she would look in her own bed in her home. Freshly painted toenails wagging in the air, maybe some music playing softly in the background on a record player twice her age. He imagined she'd smile from time to time through the story's ebbs and flows. Vincent had seen the way her expression changed when she was alone, her body flowing around the room like silk in the wind. Prudence scooped a large curl behind her ear, then nibbled on her thumbnail.

The story must be compelling.

Then her feet stopped and her eyes wandered up to the wall in front of her. Vincent sat up in his chair, leaning into the screen. She reached under her pitiful excuse for a mattress and pulled out a folded piece of paper—his note.

Tell me why, was all it said.

She looked at the camera, at him, and held it up. Vincent paused. She motioned for him to come, still looking at the camera. He couldn't resist. He grabbed a pad and pen before rushing out the door. When he reached her cell door, he watched her stand, then mime for the pen and paper. He hurriedly slid them through the slot. She wrote on the pad and returned a page to him.

Can we talk in the shower room?

I don't feel like writing notes.

Vincent looked up from the note and caught her eyes staring at him through the window on her door. Her eyes were devoid of any longing, like before. She mouthed the word "please." Without hesitation, he unlocked the door and entered, cuffing her as he did. *Stupid* and *fool* sounded loudly in his brain as he walked her to the shower room. Not a word was spoken, not a movement out of line.

Once they were inside, Vincent hesitantly gestured for her wrist, which she set in his hands. He briefly looked down at her hands, noticing how out of place they were in the shackles. Gently, he removed one cuff and then linked it to the wall behind her. He waited for her to speak.

Prudence popped each of her fingers with her thumb and took a deep breath. "I understand you must feel slighted, but I was in a different frame of mind the other night."

"Elaborate," he said, folding his arms.

"In a sense, Vincent, I used you." His name dropped from her tongue like an unwanted sour candy. "You wouldn't understand."

"Help me understand. Because from where I stand, from what I've heard, you sound like a nympho." His jaw tensed. He hated having used Benitez's choice of word to describe her. His eyes searched her face, concerned while simultaneously admiring her beauty. Being this close to her, close enough to touch her, made his knees weak.

"What do you mean by what you've heard, Vincent?" she asked, not looking his way. Despite her displeasure at having such a conversation, she felt like he deserved an explanation. Just how much she was willing to disclose with him was unclear.

"Officer Benitez is going around telling everyone that you two previously had...*relations*."

"I'm surprised that it wasn't spread long before now, based on what little I know of him," she said matter of factly.

Vincent gulped hard. "So, you're not denying it?"

"I'm not keen on lying, you understand. Now, what point are you trying to reach, exactly?" she asked, her eyes finally meeting him.

"Why do you sleep with random men? What's wrong with you?" he questioned, coming unraveled. A smile flickered across Prudence's face. He was jealous.

Endearing.

"Believe me, it is no choice of mine, if that's what you think."

"Not your choice?" Annoyance smoldered in his throat. "Did you moonlight as an escort? Did working as an accountant not pay enough, Prudence?"

Her brow furrowed at his knowledge about her profession. She wondered if Vincent had been researching her. She certainly hadn't disclosed any of her personal information with him, or anyone for that matter, since she arrived. It was true, however, that starting with her conversation with Gerty, she was allowing herself to open up today without any inkling as to why.

How much does he know?

"Again, *Vincent*, you wouldn't understand," she said, suddenly feeling very defensive. "I have certain desires that strike me from time to time. Fucking isn't always what sedates these impulses, but sometimes they are so intense, it's the best way out. Solitary, it seems, isn't the ideal place for such a thing to arise."

The crease in Vincent's brow deepened as he continued to listen, trying his best to understand though disbelief was clouding his better judgement.

"This is why I was running for hours on end in my cell, touching myself relentlessly. It's like a hunger that isn't quenched by simply snacking."

She was pouring her heart out to him. "When these desires are mild, I can usually just do as I've mentioned, or go for a hike or speed down a rural road in the country as fast as my vehicle can go. Anything to expel the pent-up adrenaline that takes me over. Once the desires are soothed, I go about my life." Prudence caught a glimpse of concern in his eyes just then, maybe even worry for her. She quickly looked away.

"But you must have someone—family? Someone who's there to support you when you feel this way?" Vincent asked. As he moved in closer, he noticed her starting to distance herself. Distressing tension filled the space between them.

He knows nothing at all.

"I don't long for social communications in my current state and don't crave any physical interaction with anyone," she snapped, backing into the wall to which she was cuffed.

"But why?"

"What do you want from me?" Prudence could feel her heart race and heat rise in her face. Vincent stepped closer, offering his hand to comfort her, but she jerked away. She felt like she was suffocating.

Why is this happening?

"It's just how I am! If it were up to me, Vincent, I would choose to not feel anything at all times! If it were up to me…," She looked back up at him finally. His face read defeat and, for some reason, her heart ached.

"...I wouldn't continue to confuse poor men like you, or have done what

I did to get here. But such is life. Always *exactly* what you don't want it

to be. So forgive me for being cold, but I simply prefer it this way."

He waited a moment, trying to process what she was saying, but spoke

before he could thoroughly grasp it. He couldn't help it. He was hurt.

"So, you never wanted me. Never felt anything."

She shook her head, slightly disappointed in his response. "No one can

ever understand."

CHAPTER 11

December 2018

A loud knocking echoed through her apartment. Gretchen must have heard Prudence sprint by her door. Prudence was in a full sweat, her clothes clinging to her as if she had just emerged from a pool.

"Ms. Malkin?" *Knock, knock.* "Are you in?"

Prudence's upper lip twitched in a snarl, agitated that Gretchen would ask such a moronic question after obviously having heard her run by.

The knocking and Gretchen's shrill voice persisted through the door as Prudence tore off her coat and discarded it on the sofa. Her body was pulling her to the door, to answer it, to quiet the noise. Her mind fought as hard as it could to stop herself and remain quiet until Gretchen left.

But when her eyes opened, she was standing in front of the door, her hand on the knob.

Her heart pounded furiously as she turned it, her mind screaming for her to stop, but her hand persevered, opening the door anyway.

"Oh!" Gretchen sounded startled. "Ms. Malkin, are you alright? You look like you fell in the dunk tank at a carnival."

Prudence forced a small smile. "Prudence, Ms. Hale, *just* Prudence. As always."

She moved to the side to allow Gretchen in. Her landlady stepped inside and looked around for a seat before finding one at the dining room table. She planted herself in one of the chairs that surrounded it, tightening her scraggly ponytail, which sat at the crown of her head. Her cheeks were rosy and sagged like those of a hound dog. Wisps of baby hair flew around her face.

"Well, *Prue*, I'm sure you can imagine why I'm here," she began.

Prudence's hands were shaking and her breathing was heavy. She was feeling even more anxious and irritable than she had felt before her meeting with Edgar and she couldn't shake it. Gretchen's voice was driving her mad as the little lady continued to drone on about "the importance of punctuality with one's affairs." Prudence stood just

behind her, responding with a single word every time Gretchen paused.

Her mind formed a vision of her beating Gretchen until she was nothing

but sludge on the floor, encasing her feet. She imagined picking up the

umbrella propped by the door, bracing Gretchen against the chair, and

shoving it violently down her throat.

"Well!" Gretchen shrieked. "Do you have rent or not?"

Prudence cocked her jaw to one side, popped each of her fingers with her

thumb, and summoned all of the composure she could muster before

she spoke.

"Of course, Ms. Hale. And I will certainly get it to you. It's just in the

kitchen. Can I fetch you some water?" Her heartbeat finally steadied.

She felt as though she could make it, at least until Gretchen departed.

She just needed to remain calm and stop entertaining her subconscious.

"That would be lovely. No ice, please. I have sensitive teeth."

"I'll return in just a moment," Prudence replied, then made her way

around the corner and into the kitchen. Internally, she begged Gretchen

not to speak another word until she returned. Silence for one singular

moment was all she needed. A stone-shaped magnet on her refrigerator

held the money order she had made out over a week ago. She grabbed it, then turned around and retrieved a glass from her cabinet. So far, so

good. Prudence switched on the filter connected to her faucet and

poured water into the glass. Her hands had ceased shaking now. Once

the glass was a little over halfway full, she shut off the faucet.

"Oh, do you have any lemon?" Gretchen called out from the dining

room.

Prudence's stomach dropped. Her hands began to tremble again and her

heart pounded.

"I take lemon in my water if you do!"

Her eyes drifted over to the knife block on her countertop. She set the

glass and money order on the counter and proceeded to draw the largest

knife in the block, running her thumb gently over the blade. It was a

little dull. It wouldn't do in its current state.

Prudence rummaged through a drawer, then retrieved a whetstone.

"My apologies, Ms. Hale, but I haven't got any lemon at the moment."

Her voice shook as she quietly sharpened the knife. The metallic sound

it made as she deliberately and steadily scraped it over the whetstone

resonated in her ears like a violin's bow coursing across its delicate

strings. She could hear her breath heavy over the music as all other

sounds drained from existence. Prudence's eyes rolled back in her head.

She firmly clenched the handle of the knife, a euphoric sensation filling her bones.

Gretchen intruded with her ear-splitting cry. "Well, then, forget the water. I really should go! I'll just take the rent money!"

Prudence snarled and her nostrils flared as she threw down the whetstone and charged into the dining room, knife in hand.

Hacking away at the poor, defenseless Gretchen Hale, Prudence reveled in the sensation of blood splattering all over her, like a warm mist from a water hose on a hot day in mid-June. She felt the strain of her impulses melt away, relieving her body of all its extra weight as she stood over her almost deceased landlady. Blood ran from her jugular like a waterfall, pouring down over her once-lilac blouse, which was almost completely torn off. Through the rich, dark blood, Prudence noticed that she had nearly severed Gretchen's left breast.

Taking in a jagged breath, Prudence conclusively felt normal once again, but as she regained her equilibrium, she knew that this was not something she was prepared to cover up. She placed the knife on Gretchen's lap and proceeded into the kitchen, where she gulped down the glass of water she had initially poured for Gretchen.

Her thirst was overwhelming.

Then she washed her hands of the thick, sticky substance she had

fantasized about moments before. Once her hands were clean, she

called 911 for the police to collect Gretchen and herself from the

apartment.

"Don't worry, I'll wait here," she said, then hung up the phone, setting

it on the counter.

Knowing it would be a while before she would have another chance to

bathe, Prudence stripped off her clothes, placed the bloodied garments

into a plastic bag she took from beneath her kitchen sink, and, without a

glance, walked naked down the hall past Gretchen's slumped-over

corpse.

When she started the water, her heart leapt with excitement. She tested

the temperature with her hand until it was just right. Prudence scrubbed

at her skin feverishly until it turned a blistering red. She watched as the

water rinsed away Gretchen's blood and the amalgamation of hers and

Edgar's sweat that had dried on her skin, both circling the drain at her

feet.

CHaPTer 12

March 2019

The gray walls lacked the magic they once possessed. Where they had once been a calming tranquil ash that evoked a sense of ease for Prudence, they were now sad and somber. The paint was chipping in the creases between the bricks, revealing deep crimson underneath, like a light shown through flesh.

The walls were alive, breathing.

They took in the thoughts, fears, and sadness of prior inmates, and those before them, who sat alone within their confines. A deep, subtle sound emitted off of them, beating like a drum, pulsating through Prudence's chest. Like an empath, the walls absorbed the inmates' sorrows and made them their own, but never freed them from it. And with each new inmate, these sensations were imprinted on them, intended to drive them mad as the walls had become. Prudence was succumbing to them too, feeling as though she were missing a fragment of herself. A void where, before, she was numb.

The clock that hung just outside her cell struck 7:00 pm when in strolled Officer Williams. He was an elderly man who, from what she understood, worked only part-time at the prison, for this was the only day she would see him. There would be no Officer Kore today, like last Saturday, but this time Prudence dreaded his absence. Vincent's absence.

When Saturday night approached, a melancholy—one that Prudence couldn't shake—engulfed her so entirely that she couldn't catch her breath. Perhaps it was because he hadn't spoken to her in the days following their last encounter. She had grown accustomed to his presence, his voice, but then, after she had revealed some of the secrets behind her lasciviously driven urges, he hadn't so much as looked at her. Prudence hadn't noticed him glance at her door during his rounds nor had she felt his gaze that, to her surprise, warmed her in a way she had never felt.

Like she was safe. Wanted.

To her dismay, she found herself missing him. It had been so long since she had missed someone, she had forgotten the soul-crushing sensation of it. Like he was a limb missing from her body, one that she desperately needed to scratch. In the past, many men or self-proclaimed friends had shown affection and love to her, but she simply couldn't bring herself to return the same devotion to anyone. In addition to missing him, she felt guilty for having made him endure the torment she knew her presence and initiations caused him. His hold on her that night in the showers, though forceful, was cautious. Even as he squeezed her neck, she could feel restraint, fully aware of his strength. He was clearly very in tune with her pleasure and received his own only as a secondary thought.

He *wanted* her to feel good.

And then his immediate concern for her when they had finished told her even more. He was interested in more than sex—yet another concept she was not privy to. Her heart ached and her loins burned for him. Prudence had never possessed such feelings unaccompanied by her raging affliction and she wasn't sure how to handle them.

She was having dreams about Vincent now, vivid dreams containing images of his body, their passionate encounter, his eyes that traced over her so carefully so that he could absorb every detail of her skin. Her entire being craved Vincent, his presence, his touch, his gaze. Maybe she could capture his attention after a while. Maybe she hadn't completely soiled their bond.

Damn these walls.

◆

The smell of seared, hand-ground lamb filled Vincent's nostrils, infusing him with the fervor of his childhood. He reminisced about running through the kitchen, causing a ruckus as his mother hollered after his father to capture him. From the kitchen, he would make his way into the living room, running past his father who still sat in his chair in front of the television, having not heard his wife, who was now shaking her wooden spoon at him. Splatter from hot lamb fat speckled his shirt.

Vincent was seated in front of the island in the center of his mother's kitchen, watching her chop eggplant for her famous moussaka. The fleeting memory brought a light smile to his face. The kitchen was warmly lit. His mother's skin glowed caramel in the light. Her hair was a chrome silver and her horn-rimmed glasses slid to the end of her nose as she vigorously chopped away. Using the knife and her opposite hand, she scooped up the diced eggplant and brought it to the stove, releasing it into a hot, oil-coated pan. The eggplant sizzled when it met the pan, lightly bouncing up and down in the heated oil.

Reducing the heat, his mother turned, throwing a kitchen towel over her shoulder, and looked at her dear son. She pushed her glasses up the bridge of her nose and frowned. Her eyes were smoldering. The creases in her forehead deepened and her lips were tight.

"Ti symvaínei?" she asked.

"What do you mean? I'm fine, Ma." Vincent sat up straighter in his seat, having noticed he was slouching. She discouraged slouching.

His mother's eyes narrowed at him as she relaxed her face and said, "Fine? You think your mother doesn't notice when something is wrong with her one and only child? Ha!" She shook her red, painted finger at him, her bracelets jingling as she did. "Miló, Vincent."

"Ma, I am speaking, I am. Just haven't felt myself lately," he confessed, picking up a plump tomato and taking a bite. The tomato popped audibly between his teeth. Its juices flowed down his chin before she took it from his hands to chop, wiping his face with her towel.

"You'll ruin dinner." She chopped silently for a few moments, then removed the eggplant once it started to get golden brown. Next, she threw in the potatoes and onions with a few dashes of salt and pepper. "Grab the glass dish from the cabinet, please. I don't feel like grabbing the stepping stool," she told him as she stripped a twig of fresh thyme over the cooking vegetables.

Vincent did as his mother requested, reaching for the cabinet just above the refrigerator to retrieve her dish with ease. He grabbed the olive oil from beside the stove and stood next to her to coat the pan with it. He remembered many evenings assisting his mother in this way, learning how to cook as she did, preparing banquet-like meals for visiting family and friends.

On one such occasion, they cooked to celebrate his father's retirement from the police force. They slaved for days peeling potatoes, chopping vegetables, marinating meats of many varieties, rolling dough. Vincent's hands were chalky from flour and smelt of garlic.

"Vincent, you're not speaking," she reminded him, looking up over her glasses, which were slightly foggy from the steam rising from the pan of simmering lamb and tomatoes.

"I'm sorry. I just needed to get away. And who's better to get away and see than my mother?" He smirked at her slyly, knowing she would be moved.

His mother smiled, pushed her glasses back up her nose, and reached across the island to pat his cheek. "And nothing makes me happier. So, what has got you so down, o gios mou?"

Vincent hesitated. No matter how close he felt to his darling mother, he knew he couldn't share such subject matter with her. Couldn't tell her that he had become infatuated with a criminal at the prison where he worked, nor that he'd had sex with her in the shower after hours.

As he mulled over what to say next, his mother took the dish from him and set it on the counter beside the stove, filling it with the contents of the pans on the red, blazing burners. She layered the contents, evening them out with the back of her wooden spoon, coated in lamb fat. Once she was through, she left it to rest.

"I've had a woman on my mind," Vincent finally divulged.

His mother's eyes widened and her red-tinted lips curled in the corners. "Oh? And where did you meet her?"

"Work..." He scratched the back of his neck.

"Ah. That is how your father and I met, remember? It isn't always bad like they say, romance at work," she went on, glancing lovingly at a photo of his father on the door of the refrigerator. His father, before he finished boot camp, had worked on the grill at a family-owned Greek restaurant—her family. She was working as a door hostess when he walked in to apply. Upon learning her father had given him the job, she had begged to be moved to the kitchen. She was 19.

"I know, but it can't work like it did for you and Dad, Ma," Vincent admitted as he made his way back to his seat.

"What do you mean? Why not?" Her brow furrowed as she turned to set the oven to preheat.

"It's complicated," he admitted.

She slammed the wooden spoon on the island. "She's married!"

"No!" Vincent buried his face in his hands. "She's not married, Ma."

"Then what is stopping you? Invite her out," she declared, picking the spoon back up and setting it on the spoon rest.

"She doesn't...go out."

His mother scoffed, putting her hand on her hip. "Neither do I. Maybe you can visit her at her home. You could have a little chit-chat and watch a movie. Just don't *do* anything."

"Ma!"

"What? I know you're a man now, latreia mou. I'm sure you have sex.
But I'm still your mother and I think you should be careful." She waved
her hand at him.

Vincent's face was in his hands once again. He was imagining what she
would say if he told her that they'd already had sex and that it was
unprotected. She would have launched the perfectly packed dish of
moussaka at his head, spewing vulgarities in her native tongue about
how disgraceful and horrid he had been.

The last time he had seen her so filled with rage was when the doctor
diagnosed his father with leukemia. When the doctor told her that
nothing could be done about his condition at its advanced stage. When
the doctor said he must have been in excruciating pain for a very long
time. Vincent remembered looking at her through the window on the
door of the dim hospital room as he sat at his father's bedside. His
mother was enraged, pointing her red-painted finger in the doctor's
face, baring her teeth as she spat obscenities at him—words most likely
intended for Vincent's father.

Vincent held his father's hand as he lay there, tubes up his nose and
down his throat, IVs in the bend of his arm, wearing a gown much too

big for his fragile, pale body. He had noticed his father withering away more and more each time he came to visit, but didn't think much of it. Vincent thought it was the old age that was beginning to take hold, pulling his father's skin from its frame as the weight put on by years of retirement dropped off. Blanching it, covering it in tiny red dots. Old age making it so delicate that the slightest bump would bruise it, tear it, make it bleed. Thinking back on it now, he wondered how they could have been so blind.

The medication flowing into his veins was intended to keep him asleep, keep him calm and free from distress as his body and soul succumbed to the disease. Thankfully so, Vincent thought, for if his father was able to hear his wife through that door, he would become thoroughly unraveled. Tears streamed down Vincent's face as he watched his mother's rage melt into sorrow. She clutched the patient doctor who, despite his full schedule, remained to console her.

They'd been married for 35 years.

"It doesn't matter anyway because she told me she wasn't interested...in so many words," Vincent said, scraping dirt from beneath his fingernails out of her line of sight. He hadn't washed his

hands as well as he should have when she'd asked him to.

"Not interested? And why not?"

"She said I couldn't understand her, that no one could," he answered.

His mother checked her watch for the time, then slid the baking dish

into the pre-heated oven.

"Then make her see that you're willing to try." She was emulsifying

some flour and butter now, preparing the béchamel.

He said, "I've tried. But what little she told me about herself *was* hard to

understand. She was right."

"Then you aren't trying hard enough," his mother replied, leaning

against the island, her hand on her hip again. "To actually try

understanding someone else, you have to rid your mind of what makes

sense to you and open it to what makes sense to them. You cannot

understand someone when your mind is too clouded by your own

experiences. Learn her experience, her life. Learn what makes her who

she is. Then you can understand." His mother put the dish in the oven,

then turned to face him. "How do you think I came to forgive your

father?"

"Ma, Dad was sick. It's not his fault he got sick," Vincent countered,

looking up into her eyes. It was like looking into a mirror.

"He could have said something. Could have gone to see a doctor, gotten

help. But he didn't, and you know why? Because that's how your father

was." She removed her glasses, letting them hang against her breast,

both hands on the island now. The wound was ripping open at what had

been a seamless scar like it was brand new.

"Did you know that his mother died from consumption when he was a

boy?" Vincent shook his head no. "Doctors came and went, came and

went, came and went. But there was nothing they could do for her. Your

grandfather was so consumed by anguish, he would have done anything

to help her. He uprooted his family, your grandmother, your father, all

of his siblings, and moved them from Greece to America. When they

examined her at the border and came to the obvious conclusion that she

was sick, they turned her, and *only* her, away. Your grandfather begged!

Begged them to treat her, begged them to cure her at any cost. Offered

them money, family relics, his own *life* for hers. And as he begged, your

grandmother, so sick and tired from the long journey they took to get

here, collapsed and died…Right in front of your father." Her eyes welled up as she spoke. She finished the sauce in silence, then poured it over the moussaka, which she placed back in the oven.

"Your father was the eldest of four. He saw it all and held onto it. His father going mad with grief, his mother's struggle to get better. He wouldn't have that for me, he wouldn't have me become his father and wouldn't have that for you. In understanding your father, I found peace. With that peace, I knew it was his only way." Vincent was shocked and so taken by his mother's sorrow that he quickly embraced her. Though she cried into his chest, she made no sound. Vincent stroked his mother's hair, holding her firmly. Her hair shimmered in the light, etched with her wisdom and strength. She sniffed twice, then pulled away from his hold, looking up into his eyes.

"Ma, thank you. I'm sorry if I upset you," he finally said.

"Ah. This old lady will learn not to cry so much one day," she said, waving her hand, making her bracelets jingle. "I think people don't give the heart as much credit as it is due. For all that it can take and yet still stay together enough to keep us alive. It's amazing." She looked down at her watch as she made her way back around the island to open the oven and check on dinner.

CHaPTer 13

Eyes wide, heart galloping in her chest, Prudence couldn't contain her composure when she saw a note slide under her door. She hurried toward the door to retrieve the piece of paper, then looked out the window to see Vincent's face, but he wasn't there. She hesitated a moment, leaning into the window to peer around the sides of her cell door, but he wasn't waiting as he had done before. Suddenly, her excitement about the note morphed into dread, as she feared what it could mean.

She looked down at it in her hands. It was folded haphazardly, as if he'd been rushing, the creases uneven and worn on the edges. With trembling hands, Prudence unfolded the note.

Why do you hate your name?

Prudence blinked rapidly, perplexed wondering why he would ask this. Still holding the note, she backed into her bed frame and sat down, searching for an answer to his question. She knew why, but how to tell him—if she decided to tell him—caused her apprehension.

Vincent quickly returned to the orderly station. He knew she'd need a moment to think over her response, but was overwrought with anxiety about what she would say. He sat in the swivel chair at the counter, scratching the back of his neck as he pondered her answer, worried she'd say something he couldn't handle again.

He'd written the note on a page taken from a notepad at his mother's house. After their talk, and as she finished plating their dinner, he wrote down his question for Prudence. He could have asked her to expand on her "impulses" or asked how many partners she had taken, but neither of those seemed relevant to learning who Prudence Malkin was. He figured, given her clear disdain for her surname, this was a good place to start.

After writing the short note, he quickly folded the small piece of paper and slid it into his pants pocket. The following day, he transferred it into his trousers for work, but when he walked up to her cell on that day, he couldn't bring himself to give it to her. For the next two days, he would repeat this process: taking out the note to give to her, slipping it back into his pocket, and transferring it to the next pair of pants the following day. Vincent watched her each night on the monitor after he failed to give her the note. Prudence expressed signs of immense sorrow, which was very unlike her. In her first few days, she danced about in her cell, hummed cheerily, exhibited a sense of pure tranquility in being alone. For the past week, however, she had not danced and had not hummed.

The night before, Gerty had asked him if Prudence had taken any showers lately.

"No. Hasn't she gone with you?" he asked.

"Nope. And she's not eating again." Gerty shook her head.

Vincent's stomach dropped. "Not eating as in no food at all or just a little like before?"

"You know, just a nibble here and there. That girl has me throwing out so much food. And before you ask, I haven't been giving her any milk. I'm just getting worried about her."

Vincent turned on the monitor and switched through each camera before coming upon hers. She remained at her place on her bed, holding the note he gave her. After a while, she rose and began to pace from one gray wall to the other, discarding the note onto the bed as she did. Prudence was afraid that what she said would compel him to not speak to her again. She didn't want to frighten him as she clearly had before, but she couldn't bring herself to lie.

These last few days had been the most frustrating, convoluted ones she had endured in a long time. For years, she had been comfortable with her routine. Though her condition disrupted it from time to time, she was content being alone. Content being disconnected from those around her, even found she had a sense of pride because she didn't need the reassurance or comfort of other people. She never feared losing anyone because she didn't need anyone.

Prudence looked up at the camera in the top corner of her room, hoping he would be watching, and mimed a pen and paper. Moments later, she heard the door to the orderly station open, then close. As the sound of his footsteps drew nearer to her cell, her heart pounded profusely. Then he appeared. His smoldering eyes warmed her immediately and a tear formed in the corner of her eye. Vincent knelt to the ground, slid a notepad and pen under her door, and rose again.

He'd allowed his beard to grow half an inch more, she noticed, remembering how it had tickled her.

She retrieved the supplies from the ground and wrote quickly, then tore the page from the pad and pressed the note against the window for him to see.

My parents were unkind.

She removed the note so that she could see his face. His brows were furrowed but he didn't appear surprised. Not yet. He motioned for the pad, so she promptly returned it.

How so? he wrote, then slid the pad back under the door. Prudence was beginning to feel anxious.

"It's a long story," she spoke aloud, her eyes glazing over.

Vincent nodded, then walked away. She panicked, pressing her face against the window to see where he had gone. Her pride had completely dissipated in his presence. Deep down, she was scolding herself for possessing such feelings, for pitifully displaying herself in such a manner of desperation. But, much like she was when her impulses arose, she couldn't keep herself from exemplifying her pathetic, consuming need for his attention.

Vincent soon returned with a fresh set of clothes under his arm, as well as a towel and washcloth. Prudence smiled up at him just as her cell door swung open and he walked inside. He could feel her tremble when he grabbed her hands and cuffed them, then led her to the shower, closing them inside.

"It was brought to my attention that you've been refusing showers again," Vincent said, the rumble of his voice resonating in her ears. "Are you alright?"

Prudence brought her cuffed hands to her mouth and pressed her fingers to her lips; she felt embarrassment redden her face. Vincent set down the linen in his arms and approached her, took her wrists in his hands, and removed the cuffs completely.

"I know you hate being dirty," he said, walking past her to turn on the showerhead jutting out from the tiled wall. Prudence looked down at her wrists, noting that he hadn't left one of them unshackled.

"Remove your clothes, Prudence. Please." She did as she was asked, her eyes flickering toward him. Not once did he look away. Compassion bubbled up in his eyes as he watched her, not out of pity for her, as she would first think, but out of genuine concern. As she walked over to the hamper to discard her clothes, Vincent tested the water with his hand to make sure it was warm enough for her. Then he picked up the washcloth and pumped soap into his palm. Prudence walked underneath the flow of the heated water, drenching herself in it completely, running her fingers through her hair. Vincent lathered the soap into the washcloth between his hands, watching her sigh with contentment.

"Thank you, Vincent," she finally said, her eyes opening to the image of him standing directly in front of her, washcloth in hand.

"Will you let me wash you?" he asked. She looked him over, lips pouting as water dripped from them, then nodded "yes." Prudence turned her back to him, sweeping her hair over her right shoulder. Vincent rested one hand on her and began to bathe her with the other. Her eyes fluttered shut as she let herself be consumed by his tender caresses.

Tingling all over, she curled her toes and bit her lip trying to suppress a smile, to no avail. He could feel her body relax beneath his touch as he moved over her shoulders and down her arms.

"I take it you're still looking for a more fulfilling answer to your question." Prudence spoke low.

He took her hand and turned her so that she was facing him. "Only when you're ready to talk about it," Vincent replied.

"For what purpose are you asking?" she persisted.

He took her hair and scooped it over her shoulder, then traced his fingers over her collarbone. "Am I making you uncomfortable, Prue? If I am, I won't be persistent."

"No. The exact opposite, actually," she said. She reached down and grabbed his hand, which was still clutching the washcloth, and brought it to her chest, beckoning for him to continue bathing her. He proceeded to wash her chest, gently lathering her breast, lingering over her areola until her nipples peaked in his palm. He missed her, despite what she had said about using him to soothe her appetite. He had felt barren since they last spoke, conflicted by what he was feeling and knowing he should leave her alone so that he could move on, as Gallagher advised.

If he were smart, he would erase her, remove himself from her emotionally and return to reality. But as he washed her stomach and upper thighs, looking into her glassy eyes, he knew she needed him even though she claimed that she didn't. He just knew.

He proceeded to gently wash her delicate petals with the warm water on his bare fingers.

"I choose not to remember much of my childhood, Vincent," she began, clutching at his forearm. She had made up her mind. "What I'm about to tell you is rather upsetting for people to hear. Are you...are you sure you have prepared yourself for this?"

Vincent, despite a surge of uneasiness in his stomach, said he was.

"I couldn't tell you how old I was when father began letting his friends, or so I thought of them to be, come into my room at night. I would scream for him to stop them as he stood just outside the door, his feet preventing the hall light from entering my room. He never answered my pleas. After a while, I stopped pleading."

Vincent continued to bathe her, washing her neck, keeping a reassuring touch on her at all times as she continued. It was apparent that this wouldn't be an easy story for her to share. Her body was tense and rigid as she continued.

"The mornings after these visits from various men, Mother would scold me for being filthy. As if I had simply rolled in the mud outside, then came in to sit at the table. She wouldn't feed me until I bathed thoroughly. When the teachers started asking questions about the bruises on my neck and arms, it wasn't long before my parents pulled me out of school. That was when Father began taking me *to* his friends. Sometimes it was a residence, other times a motel whose clerk turned a blind eye and deaf ear to what was happening to me." Prudence was so still, looking down at the ground as she spoke, chewing at the inside of her cheek. She focused on the water pooling around her feet and descending into the drain just beneath them.

"This went on for years, until one night, when I was 14, on our way back home after leaving the motel, I kicked something hard on the floorboard with my foot after I entered the car. My parents heard nothing. I felt around with my foot to find what I had hit, then pulled it toward me, lifting it off the ground. It was a crowbar that Father had left there. I looked up at Mother and Father, who rode in silence, Mother counting the money I had earned *them* that evening. Her yellow-stained nails sifted through the bills. 'This isn't enough,' she said to Father." Prudence shook her head. "*Not enough.*"

Vincent was still, his hand holding her wrist.

"I felt the end of the crowbar, just opposite the curve. It was slightly rusted. I remember I was able to rub off bits of sediment from its rough point. Then, with great force, I impaled the back of Mother's head with it. I don't remember if Father said anything. All I could hear was a choking sound coming from Mother. It was difficult to retrieve the crowbar from her head, as it had gone through her right eye socket. When I finally had it, Mother slumped over. Father was reaching back at me, trying to get the tool away from me, swerving on the road as he did. I never understood why he hadn't just pulled over. I hit his hand with the bloodied tool. Then, with the curved end, I hooked it around the side of his face, piercing his temple. I pulled as hard as I could until it was lodged deep in the side of his head. I remember being confused because he continued to move, directionless, gasping for air. He ran the car into the side of the median on the highway. The car rolled five times."

She looked up at Vincent at last. Tears had formed in their eyes, and his mouth was agape. Prudence took his hand and brought it up to the base of her neck, then pushed his fingers in through her damp hair. "Around there is a scar where an incision was made to relieve the pressure on my brain post-accident."

His fingers grazed over the scar.

"I was placed in a juvenile detention center for the remainder of my teenage years. There, a psychiatrist attempted to help me with my trauma, but I didn't benefit from these sessions. You see, I was dead when they pulled me from the wreckage and even though I awoke in the hospital I would remain dead from then on. Thanks to my parents...the Malkins."

Prudence searched his eyes for a time. He was sad for her and she didn't want that.

"Will you disappear again?" she asked, the rosy hue in her cheeks fading.

He wiped away a tear with the back of his hand. The water was still running, beating against Prudence's back. Vincent reached out to shut it off when Prudence grabbed his hand in desperation.

"Please don't go."

"I'm right here. I'm sorry for everything that happened to you, Prue," he said, at a loss for the right thing to say. He knew that her story should sicken him, but all he felt was empathy as tears trailed down his face for the pain she had endured. He shut off the water and wrapped her in a towel. They stood there a moment in silence, the sound of dripping water echoing in their ears.

"Don't be. I'm not anymore. I made a life for myself and had no trouble. Until most recently, of course. I am, undoubtedly, plagued by an affliction I myself don't fully understand. Maybe if I had given that psychiatrist a chance, I wouldn't be...here." Her face contorted. Vincent embraced her. She buried her face into his chest as the warmth of his body enveloped hers. She felt heavy in his arms as her burdens presented themselves for the mass that they were. Once her body stopped shaking, Vincent released her and gave her a consoling smile. Prudence paused for a moment, looking at him in utter disbelief.

She fully expected him to run out the door in terror upon learning that she had butchered her parents. As a young girl, she had felt she had no choice, that there was no other way out.

But being here with him now, the way he embraced her, was unlike anything she had ever experienced. Too long had she carried the weight of her past alone. Now she felt that she had found someone to help relieve some of the pressure. For the first time, she thought, this must be what having a family felt like.

Unconditional love.

Lifting her hand to his face, she stroked his beard, her thumb tracing his bottom lip.

"I'm crazy about you…You know that?" Vincent's hot breath brushed over her thumb as he spoke.

Lifting herself on the tips of her toes, Prudence captured his lips with her own, wrapping her arms around his neck, her towel falling to the floor. Though her still-wet body further dampened his uniform, Vincent pulled her flesh against him, kissing her back deeply. He was completely captivated by her. Though he feared where this would lead him, he let himself succumb to her. He held her up, lifting her feet from the ground, kissing her again.

Her legs wrapped around his waist, anchoring herself to him. Vincent kissed across her neck, nibbling here and there. His hands gripped her bottom, then trailed up her waist and back. Eyes closed, Prudence rested her cheek on the side of his face, moaning softly into his ear. She slid down his torso until her feet hit the ground. He breathed heavily as he watched her, her large, lustrous eyes fixated on his. First, she rubbed the front of his groin to feel him harden before she pulled it out and took his girth into her hands. She stroked slowly and deliberately. His eyes were heavy as he tried to maintain their gaze. Prudence knelt and licked the head of his cock, then up from the base of the shaft, making him tremble. Her mouth was so warm over him that when she pulled him out, the air of the room was excruciatingly cold.

Her momentum quickened, pulling him closer to the edge as he grabbed a handful of her hair in an attempt to slow her pace, fearing he'd cum too quickly. Clutching at his thighs, which tightened and quaked beneath her grasp, Prudence moaned on his cock, relishing the way he felt and tasted.

The vibrations of her muffled moan coursed through him so violently, he pulled her off him and stood her on her feet, then plunged his tongue into her mouth and bit her lip. As he drank from her lips, Prudence unbuttoned his shirt and ran her fingers over his chest and arms, sliding the shirt off. Vincent pulled off his undershirt, his bare flesh steaming hot against hers. He lifted her once more, slowly sinking his cock into her.

He pushed her back against the wall, grasping her thighs, and held her still as he pounded into her dripping wet petals. Their breathing was heavy, their hearts beating ferociously in unison. Prudence crumbled in his arms as she came the first time, then the second, squeezing tight around his cock. She arched her back, allowing Vincent to capture one of her nipples in his mouth, lapping away at the tight bud. She whimpered, unable to keep quiet as he drove her to complete madness. Squeezing tightly around her waist, slowing his pace, Vincent groaned, then pulled out of her. His legs felt weak, but still he held her in his arms above the ground, deeply inhaling the scent of her skin. Prudence rested her head on his shoulder, kissing it softly.

Reluctantly, Vincent cuffed her. After they dressed, he returned her to her cell. As he walked back to the orderly station, he glanced into the inmates' rooms. All were asleep, including Collins. He sat in the swivel chair and retrieved his phone from beneath a stack of papers, sending a text to Gallagher:

1:56 am

Vincent: Gritty's tonight?
Gallagher: They closed at 1.
Vincent: Beers at my place?
Gallagher: Uh oh…

CHAPTER 14

February 2008

A faint aroma of lavender filled the harvest orange-tinted room

where Prudence sat on a brown suede chaise lounge. On the walls of the

office hung framed abstract art along with certifications and family

photos. A massive bookshelf, stuffed to the brim with books and various

knick-knacks, covered a wall adjacent to where she sat. The window

beside her was covered with a sheer purple drape that was completely

incapable of keeping out any amount of light. Rain streamed down like

small rivers on a map. From the windows, Prudence could feel a chill

that pierced the warmth in which this stuffy office attempted to cloak

her.

"Prudence?" said a soft, velvety voice. Dr. Phyllis Taylor sat patiently

across from Prudence. "Would you like to speak a little bit with me

today?"

"I don't know," she replied, tracing the small streams on the window,

peeking briefly at Dr. Taylor's reflection in the glass.

She was an older lady with hair very obviously dyed an orangey-blonde,

held up by a vintage hairpin adorned with a gaudy amber stone.

Prudence also noticed that she repeatedly licked her bottom lip,

smearing her red lipstick so much that a large brown freckle was visible

through it.

"Well, if you want," Dr. Taylor continued, "we can start by talking about

your parents. I think it is very important that we flesh out the struggle

you had with them at such a young age so that you can properly heal

from your...difficult experiences. Don't you?"

"How should I know? I'm still a child." She popped her fingers with her

thumb underneath her crossed arms, turning her body away from the

doctor and toward the window.

"Yes, you could say 14 is still considered a child, but you've also reached

what is called adolescence. This is a time in a young individual's life when they are maturing from a child into an adult. This is a crucial time for your growth as a young woman."

"I don't want to talk to you. Can I go now?"

Dr. Taylor's brow furrowed. Worry etched across her face as she stood from her seat.

"I really hope you will open up to me in one of these sessions, Prue. I can help you, but not if you won't let me."

Fury burned at the back of Prudence's eyes as she glared at the doctor.

"No one was there to help me when I actually needed it, so I helped myself. Now that I don't need help, you want to pretend that you forcing me to talk about things I don't want to talk about is going to change anything."

"Prudence." Dr. Taylor removed her glasses. "Holding in all of this pain will only make you worse. You have to let it out."

"No, I don't." Prudence rose from her seat, grabbed her backpack, and rushed out the door.

St. Joan's Juvenile Detention Center in Syracuse, New York wasn't exactly home to the poster children for successful delinquent adolescents. Prudence could tell she would join the ranks of fruitless cases upon her leaving for refusing treatment. She didn't want their help or false sympathy. They wanted to be able to tell the world how great their facility was for nursing a battered girl back to life after such traumatic circumstances, but Prudence was not going to be that girl.

It had been just under eight months since she had arrived there and that was the very first time she had spoken at any length with Dr. Taylor. In her very first session, the old bat had asked her, "Do you miss your parents?"

Prudence didn't even grimace with the annoyance she felt bubbling in her gut at being asked such an asinine question. She could feel Dr. Taylor searching her face for a response—a response she was determined not to give her, no matter how compassionate and caring her rhetoric sounded. Further, Prudence couldn't fathom why she would miss her parents.

Early on, when the abuse first began, Prudence remembered missing them in their life before. She missed the smell of Mother's hand lotion as she tucked Prudence into bed, lingering on her sheets, filling her little nose. She missed the stubble on Father's chin when he tickled her incessantly and smothered her in itchy kisses. She missed the small nuances of her life then that gave off the illusion that she was loved.

In the first year, she was terrified of "bedtime," as if somehow that was
what was causing her misfortune.

"Mother?" she would say. "Can't we watch one more episode? Maybe a
movie next!"

"No, Prudence. You know Father has a friend coming by in a few
minutes," Mother would reply. "You'll have to be in bed by then."

It crushed her.

It took Prudence a long time to realize that it wasn't the night that
brought them. And yet, when she realized it was, in fact, Mother and
Father, she rationalized by telling herself that they needed money and
that this was her way of helping. She told herself that they loved her and
wanted to take care of her, but needed her help. And because she loved
them, she felt obligated to tolerate the abuse like a good girl, so she
never complained. But when she was taken out of school and more
regularly forced to perform illicit sexual favors, she was convinced they
didn't love her. She made herself return that same heartless gesture.
She stopped begging for their attention, stopped saying she loved them,
stopped speaking altogether. When she wasn't beneath a client, she
spent her time alone in her room, reading books that distracted her and
made her believe, if only for a few hours, that she was somewhere else.

But sadly, every time a book ended and she lifted her eyes from its pages, she was back in her room, with a man waiting at the door, his shoes blocking the hall light.

Dr. Taylor would never understand, even if she decided to "let her in," as she would always remark. Prudence knew that every story she relayed would be met with empty apologies and empty promises of safety. She didn't want any of the doctor's pity and loathed the idea of her celebrating about getting her to talk. She could hear Dr. Taylor's voice in her head, saying, "That wasn't too bad, was it?" or "I think we're making progress!" It was bad, and someone else knowing about the atrocities in her life was not progress, not in Prudence's eyes. It wouldn't make what happened disappear and heal what had broken into such fine pieces that an attempt to fuse them back together would be impossibly hopeless.

It wouldn't bring her parents back to life, nor would it make her wish she hadn't killed them.

Prudence was glad they were dead, glad she did it because no one else was doing anything to stop them. She didn't need Dr. Taylor and St. Joan's Juvenile Detention Center's version of aid. She needed only herself.

It was early, but because she left Dr. Taylor's office half an hour before her session was scheduled to conclude, Prudence decided to head to class and sit alone for a while. She had been feeling very anxious lately and these small breaks alone weren't quite as helpful as they once were in calming her nerves. When she was alone, her brain ran through the long list of demons that plagued her.

One thought that remained prevalent was the memory of her parents' murders. She could feel mother's warm, sticky blood seeping down the rusted crowbar, covering her hand, mixing with bits of sediment that crumbled from the crowbar's rusted tip. She remembered how she had felt when she impaled her mother's skull—an almost immediate sensation of liberation made that much more real when she punctured her father's temple. Though she knew she had done the right thing to save herself from a seemingly endless cycle of rape, Prudence feared that she had actually enjoyed it—so much so that now she couldn't stop thinking about it. Though she was in no immediate danger, she felt the need to do it again.

She wouldn't bring this up with Dr. Taylor.

Prudence had gotten off pretty well for the murder of her parents. She feared that if she told anyone that she had liked killing them, they would lock her away for good. She didn't want that. She wanted out of here, to be on her own, to take care of herself and not have to answer to someone else ever again. She just had to figure out how to stop these feelings, but the answer eluded her.

As she sat in Mr. Travis' empty classroom, Prudence scraped the underbelly of her desk with her pencil. Hard enough to wear it down quickly, but not hard enough to break it. She was feeling very overwhelmed now, with sweat beading up on her brow. To her confusion and dismay, moisture pooled between her thighs. Her heart pounded in response to the sensation and her breathing became heavy. It was all she could do not to cry. She dropped the pencil to the ground and put her hands together between her legs, pressing against herself to soothe the throbbing.

"Prudence?"

Her cheeks burned feverishly with embarrassment and her eyes were wide as she looked up toward the doorway where Mr. Travis stood.

"Prudence, what are you doing here so early? Are you alright?" He shut the door behind him and walked toward his desk to unload his backpack with the day's assignments and his copy of the textbook. Mr. Travis

couldn't have been older than 28. His hair was like honey and his voice

was enriched with a deep melodic tone. Prudence's eyes didn't leave

him as he trekked across the room toward her. She wanted to remove

her hands from their place, but couldn't. As he drew nearer to her, she

grew more salacious.

"Are you...ok?" he asked again, towering over her desk, his eyes

examining her face before trailing down to her hands. She noticed this.

Her eyes glazed over and her eyelids hung heavy.

Her body stopped quaking, making the sound of her heartbeat even

louder in her ears.

"No...Mr. Travis. I don't think I am," she replied.

He crossed his arms and leaned against the desk behind him. She

couldn't take her eyes off his vascular forceps and the way his slacks

clung to his upper thighs. She caressed herself gently with her fingers

now. Prudence was feeling an unprecedented pull to get nearer to him.

"Tell me what's wrong. You can trust me," Mr. Travis cooed.

She smiled, "I'm sure."

Rising to her feet, pushing her breasts forward, Prudence swayed her
hips around her desk and stood so close to him, she could feel the
warmth emanating off his body.

"I'm not feeling like myself, Mr. Travis. Maybe you can help me?"

He looked down on her, a grin forming at the corner of his mouth. From
the first day she had walked into his classroom, he had been intrigued
by Prudence. She walked with so much purpose and poise, had she not
been listed on his roster, he would have thought she was a fully grown
woman.

Prudence knew, she always knew, when a man took a liking to her. It
used to terrify her. She worried that such men would take advantage of
her and make her do things she didn't want to do, as they always had
before.

But she wouldn't allow that anymore. Now she was in control.

Prudence reached up and stroked his arm gently with her moist
fingertips. He tensed slightly beneath her touch. Uncrossing his arms,
he took her hand in his and lifted her chin with the other.

"Call me Alex."

"Should I lock the door, *Alex*?" she asked, her lips pouting.

He bit his bottom lip, looked down at his watch, and nodded. His green and white striped tie flung over his shoulder, he took Prudence from behind as she leaned over his desk, her eyes fixated on a store-bought trophy that read "#1 Teacher."

It lasted less than five minutes.

When they were through, she told him she was going to the restroom and unlocked the door. She walked past a group of students headed for Mr. Travis' classroom. She felt them stare at her, having seen her come out, but she paid them no mind. Their curiosity in her was not an interest she possessed.

When she walked into the girls' restroom and locked herself in one of the stalls to clean herself with a soapy paper towel she had wetted at the sink, Prudence realized that she felt *normal.*

She thought back on the memory that had plagued her not 20 minutes before. It didn't conjure a rise at all. She realized that at the moment she became fixated on entrancing Mr. Travis, her mind abandoned all thought of her dark desires.

Prudence took a deep breath, disposed of the towel in the trash receptacle, and left the restroom, returning to class. As the lesson went on, she eased into her studies, not feeling distracted or uncomfortable with Mr. Travis' almost constant gaze. She felt slightly irritated at how obvious he was acting, but it was neither here nor there. By the end of the lesson, when the period bell chimed, everyone was quickly out the door, Prudence's name on their tongues. As Prudence made her way out, Mr. Travis stopped her.

"Prue, can I talk to you for a moment?" he asked, pausing as he watched the last student leave the classroom. "How was it—for you, I mean?" he asked.

"How was what?" she asked, not batting an eye.

"Don't play dumb, Prue," he said, looking out the door to see if anyone was lingering.

Her brow furrowed. She had never been asked how it "was for her." She actually found humor in his question and almost couldn't suppress a laugh. "Fulfilling, I think," she answered. "But I'm good now."

And with that, not waiting for his response, she walked out the door.

CHapTer 15

April 2019

Gallagher's words echoed louder in Vincent's ears than his own

footsteps did as he made his way down the hall to Warden Seifert's

office.

He had droned on to Gallagher, who could do nothing but shake his head

and sip his beer. Vincent had gotten home around 3:00 am and

Gallagher had shown up soon after with a chilled six-pack he had picked

up at the corner store on his way over.

They sat at his kitchen table and talked for over an hour about what had

transpired. The more Vincent told him, the more worried Gallagher became. But nothing he said could make Vincent see the red flags flying all around him.

"I think you might be going too deep, Vin," he said. "She's obviously dangerous."

"I know how it sounds, but I just feel for her. Clearly, throughout her entire life, no one has ever cared about her!"

While he was willing to admit that Prudence had endured more than her fair share of adversity, Gallagher felt she was more than Vincent, or any other person without psychological expertise, for that matter, could handle on their own.

Vincent had been summoned to the warden's office as soon as he entered the building. However, he hadn't considered the purpose of the meeting, so concerned was he about the conversation of the night before. Also, exhaustion heavily clouded him.

When he reached the office, the door was propped open, so he peeked inside, knocking courteously. He could see that Seifert was speaking with a man seated across from his desk, his back to Vincent. When they heard him knock, they both looked up at him.

It was Benitez, a shit-eating grin scrawled across his face. Seifert's brow furrowed and his mustache scrunched as his face contorted with disappointment. Vincent cleared his throat, his exhaustion leaving him only to be replaced by apprehension.

"Officer Benitez, if you don't mind giving us a moment." Seifert motioned toward the door. Benitez rose from his seat and walked out, slowing his pace to glare at Vincent on his way out.

"Have a seat, Kore. Shut the door please."

Vincent closed the door and hesitantly took the seat across from the desk. "Something you needed to see me about, sir?" he asked, doing everything he could to hide the fear in his voice over why Benitez had been there.

"Kore. You know I respect you. Always have," Seifert said, taking his seat with a heavy sigh.

"Yes, sir?"

"So, when a rumor about you...and a particular inmate started floating around, I paid it no mind. I hear bullshit all the time. Everyone here acts like this goddamn place is a sorority house with the amount of hot garbage that goes around," Seifert continued.

Vincent squirmed subtly in his seat. "I don't know what Benitez may have told you, but those rumors that he made up are false. He's been toying with me ever since he got back," Vincent explained, every word falling out abruptly like vomit.

Seifert shook his head and scoffed. "This has nothing to do with Benitez. Fletcher was half an hour early for his shift this morning, said he wanted to beat the snow. When he got in, you weren't at your station. He said he thought he heard you in the showers. A particular inmate was not in her cell."

"I can explain," Vincent said, feeling thoroughly panicked now. "Officer Turner told me that Malkin has been refusing showers. I know it's against policy, but she asked me if she could shower. That was it, I—"

"I checked the surveillance cameras." Seifert's mustache twitched as he brought his hands together on his desk. Vincent's heart stopped. "You wanna tell me why you were in the shower room with her for over an hour? Or why were you two passing notes under the cell door?"

Scratching the back of his neck, Vincent was unable to find the words to explain this away.

He was embarrassed, petrified even.

"I have no excuse, sir. I failed you as an officer of this facility and for that I am ashamed."

Seifert leaned back in his chair, rubbing at the stubble on his chin already coming through after that morning's shave. "I don't need to hear any details, but it better not come back that this *affair* was not consensual for both parties. The last thing I need right now is for my prison to end up on the front page of tomorrow's newspaper thanks to you deciding to stick your dick where it doesn't belong. This mess stays between you and me."

"What about Fletcher?" Vincent asked, his shoulders dropping with relief.

"I watched the security footage alone. He saw nothing," Seifert answered. "Moving forward, obviously you will be removed from solitary and I'm putting you on a two-week suspension without pay."

Vincent nodded, then immediately thought about Prue. "Who will be taking my place?" he asked.

"For now, Benitez," Seifert answered.

Vincent's nostrils flared. "Sir. I know in my position, at this point, I don't really have a say in any of your decisions, but I don't think it's such a good idea to have Benitez there."

"You're right. You don't," Seifert snapped. "He sure as shit was not my first pick by a long shot, but he needs the extra hours and is the only one with the availability. Your little girlfriend will need to learn to behave herself until I find someone else."

"But, sir—"

"This isn't up for discussion! You're the luckiest son of a bitch alive given that you're not being hauled off to jail this instant. If I were you, I wouldn't push my luck. We are done here. Report back to my office in two weeks." Warden Seifert stood abruptly and pointed to the door.

Vincent stood and headed out as instructed, but just as he grabbed the knob, he turned to Seifert and said, "You're making a huge mistake, sir. I just know it."

◆

He's late. Why is he late? Is it the weather?

Prudence's mind was riddled with thoughts laced with worry. She remembered how soaking wet Officer Turner had been when she came in. Perhaps it had continued to snow.

It was hard to tell with no windows.

The clock struck 7:23 pm when the sound of the door of the orderly's station reached her ears. She could hear a voice calling out the names of the other inmates as it made its way down the hall toward her cell.

That isn't Vincent.

"Juarez...Bell...Johnson...Velasco...Collins...Malkin!" His face came into view through her cell door and her stomach dropped. "Well, hello, Peaches."

CHAPTER 16

*B*eep.

"Vincent, it's your mother. You haven't returned my Tupperware from last week. Call me back."

Beep.

"Vincent, it's your mother, again. Call me back."

Beep.

"Vincent! Why aren't you returning my calls? Don't make me come over there!"

Beep. End of messages.

Vincent rubbed the sleep from his eyes and set his phone back on the bedside table. He felt bad for avoiding her like this, but the last couple of days, he could hardly bring himself to get out of bed. The only reason he left was to walk and feed Brocc and grab an occasional snack from the kitchen—only because he knew starvation was not the way he wished to die.

He worried day and night about Prudence, worried she thought that he had abandoned her just as she was starting to open up to him. He thought about contacting Gerty to ask if she could extend a message to Prue to let her know what had happened. But ultimately he decided it was best to not loop more people into this catastrophe he had created. Vincent had also been thinking a lot about Prue's parents and the horrendous people they were. He wondered how they could do such a thing to their own flesh and blood. It didn't take him long to start doing some research into her past. If what she said was true, there had to be a paper trail of documents and articles to prove it. Hopefully, they would help him understand why.

Vincent willed himself out of bed and flipped open his laptop. Its bright screen made his eyes ache. In the search bar, he typed "Prudence Makin" and "parents murder." There was a brief article in The Herald

Statesman that he was able to find, dated 2007, depicting the gruesome murder of "Hellions Disguised as Suburban Parents in Yonkers, NY." Vincent suddenly realized that he hadn't known where she was from; she'd made no mention of New York.

The article's wording stepped cautiously over the atrocious subject matter to avoid offending its readers, but still the story sent a chill down Vincent's spine.

"'Lara and Sam always seemed normal to me,' said Emma Belleau, a longtime neighbor of the Malkins. 'Their daughter was always so sweet, but very quiet. Reserved.'"

Vincent read that Emma had been questioned by police several times during their investigation and thought she may have known them well. He wondered if, by some slim chance, Emma still lived in the same house. He wondered what kind of perspective she'd have now years later. Maybe she remembered a small detail about the Malkins that she hadn't brought up to the police or that the press hadn't found interesting. He wondered if she could help him understand why everything happened the way it had for Prudence.

Taking a chance, Vincent searched for Emma on several social media platforms. Even after narrowing his search to only Emmas who lived in

New York, he had to look for hours through countless profile pictures of people who shared her name. He tried to match their faces to hers as pictured in the article when she'd been interviewed 12 years ago. A few looked like they could have been her, but it was difficult to tell with the added age and the lack of knowledge about whether she had moved—or passed away. In the hopes of finding the Emma Belleau he was looking for, Vincent decided to direct message all the women he felt could be her.

A knock sounded at the door, seeming to shake the apartment. Brocc pounced off his pallet and ran to the door, barking. Vincent quieted the dog, then proceeded to answer the door with caution. As he opened it, he was attacked by his own mail.

"How long has it been since you went downstairs and checked your mailbox, Vincent?" his mother yelled. "What's wrong with you, huh? No phone calls? No mail?"

"Ma, I'm sorry. How are you?" he asked, kneeling to pick up all the envelopes, cards, and advertisements she had thrown.

"How am I? I was terrified thinking about what had happened to my boy!" she said, walking in and slamming the door. Brocc ran in fear, his nails scratching on the hardwood floor as he slid across it.

"I'm thinking, is he dead? Is he hurt! Is he—is he in trouble! What!

What, o gios mou?"

His mother made her way into his kitchen, opening and closing

cabinets, assessing his groceries.

"No dishes in the sink! No food in your kitchen!"

Vincent set his mail on the counter and proceeded to the couch, his

mother following him. She set her purse beside her as she sat. He sighed

deeply and said, "Ma, I'm so sorry. I've just been here this whole time,

that's all."

She adjusted her glasses, pursed her lips, and looked him over. His

clothes were wrinkled, his facial hair unkempt, and a slight stench

exuded from his armpits.

"Did she break up with you?" she asked, meeting his eyes.

Vincent's brow furrowed. "What? Who—oh no. No, Ma."

"Did you lose your job?"

"Not exactly," he said.

His eyes trailed away and he rubbed the back of his neck where the hairs

started to stand up. His cheeks and ears burned as he pondered whether

to make up something or come clean with his mother. He knew she wouldn't stop with the questions unless he told her something. And if anything was certain, she could sense bullshit like no other.

He had to tell her.

"Ma," Vincent said, adjusting in his seat. He could see she was visibly tense, like she was trying to morph herself into a barricade, ready to fend off any form of attack. "I'm going to tell you something you aren't going to like and I just want you to know before I do that I'm not proud of any of this."

She squinted. "Ok. I'm listening."

"That woman I told you about, Prudence is her name. She's an inmate at the prison where I work," he said. His mother didn't move. Her barricade was locked up tighter than Fort Knox. "I started asking about her like you said and we got close. Very close. Our relationship was brought to the warden's attention and I was suspended for some time. I haven't lost my job, thankfully, but I'm ashamed. And most of all, I'm worried about her. That's why I haven't been answering your calls, or anyone's calls for that matter, or—"

She cut him off. "Bathing."

Vincent's shoulders sank further. He folded into himself, mortified.

She wanted to hit him in the back of the head with her purse, to shake him and scream. She was appalled, but looking at how utterly broken he was, she couldn't bring herself to break him any further. She took in a deep, jagged breath, then sighed so heavily, she half expected her lungs to fall out through her nose. Her body loosened as her barricade came tumbling down in the wake of her son's pain.

"I understand that love is love, o gios mou, but what made you do such a thing?" she asked, trying her best to remain calm though disappointment was etched across her face.

Vincent was amazed at her composure and saddened by his own self-destructive behavior. "She was...I don't know how to explain it. When I first saw her, she was the most striking woman I had ever seen. But so...cold. I had never met someone like her who could shake me the way she did. I was bewitched, Ma."

Vincent finally looked at his mother, fully expecting her to shake her head and tell him off, but she didn't. She was calm and encouraged him to continue.

"I knew that how I felt wasn't right and I did try to avoid her by moving to solitary confinement, but then, not long after, she ended up right where I was. It was like an injured bird had fallen into my hands for the second time. I felt like I had to confront my feelings. And, knowing her

as I do now, I want to help her."

"What do you know?" his mother asked.

"She's been through so much." He shook his head, "She's broken."

His mother rubbed his shoulder affectionately. "You cannot fix her,

Vincent."

He didn't argue with her about that, as he knew she was right.

Thankfully, she didn't press him further. Vincent wasn't sure how much

more he was comfortable sharing. She begged him to shower and go

grocery shopping as soon as possible, hugged him tightly, and left.

After dragging his feet to the shower, Vincent lingered under the steady

stream of water. It was a little hotter than he could usually stand, but it

was necessary to loosen the knots in his muscles brought on by stress

and lack of movement for the better part of the week. He was grateful

his mother hadn't torn him to shreds after his disgraceful confession.

Hopefully, this meant she didn't think less of him. Once he was

through, he migrated back to his bedroom to get dressed for a trip to the

store. There, on the screen of his still-open computer, he saw a new

message.

It was from Emma.

CHAPTER 17

He doesn't care about you. You're foolish to believe such fairytales.

Her heart was shattering, her legs weak as her mind beat her down

mercilessly.

Of course he cares! He might even love you!
Her head pounded, her hands shook.

You're pathetic and weak!
Tears streamed down her face like a window braced against a storm.

No, that's not true. You deserve love.
He had been gone for so long and here she was, left night after night

with the very person who had put her in solitary.

What were you thinking? How could somebody ever love you?
The confines of her small grey room were starting to suffocate her once

again, closing in on her like a trash compactor. *That's fitting.* Prudence took in several deep breaths, holding them each time before slowly

exhaling shakily in an attempt to calm herself.

Once her heartbeat steadied, she tried to rationalize what might have

happened to Vincent. Perhaps someone had discovered their

relationship—*can I call it that?*—and he'd been suspended or fired.

Maybe he asked to move to a different department or quit once he came

to his senses and realized she was insane. Prudence hoped the latter was

not the case. She was horrified to think that perhaps he used her in

some elaborate scheme just to fuck her again—but only until the

gremlin at the back of her mind reminded her about the many men *she*

had manipulated and used for a fuck over the years.

She knew, to some degree, that she had left a trail of confused and hurt

men behind her in her quest to soothe her more deadly urges. But she

always chalked it up to a deed done for the greater good. Their pain was

an unfortunate side effect. Now, however, being caught in the waves of

emotion perpetuated by what felt like rejection, she felt an even deeper

disdain for who she was.

A monster woefully undeserving of happiness.

"Prue," Gerty called through the door, preventing her train of thought

from derailing into dangerous territory yet again. "Shower time."

Prudence's already knotted stomach contorted even further. She had known this time was coming due to the now-routine string of insults that her fellow solitary inmates spewed at her door as they made their way to the shower room.

"Whore," "Bitch," Pig-loving slut."

Since word had begun to circulate that what the women had likely already speculated was happening, they must have felt justified in ridiculing her. Gerty tried in vain to silence them, but Prudence wasn't bothered by what these women thought or said. She knew, thanks to Gerty, how they'd all ended up here and couldn't be bothered with the opinions of pathetic "mommy dearests" like them.

Though she did notice that one voice—one she expected to hear amongst the many—was absent. Collins made no jests at her expense, uttered not a single word when she passed.

Even still, much worse than the heckling, "shower time" was an indicator that soon Gerty's shift would be over and Officer *Benitez* would return. His taunting had only intensified since his return from leave. Coupled with her fragile state, she could hardly bear the idea of him being close by.

On his first shift in solitary, he had threatened her for having been violent with him.

"It's just you and me in here, Peaches," he said through the door in a low, guttural tone, like a wolf stalking a rabbit. "I'll show you just how violent *I* can be."

Each day, when he made his rounds, he would remind her about the cameras and encourage her to put on a special show just for him. As he watched her in the office, when he noticed her drift off to sleep, he would walk down to her door and bang on it loudly with his baton, laughing in his maniacal chortle. Prudence barely slept. She was a constant nervous wreck, concerned he would come into her cell one of these days, invading her space. Even worse, she felt her urges bubbling up inside of her, encouraging her disquiet. Shower time with Gerty was all she had.

She needed to get clean, to maintain some semblance of normalcy, balance, and control.

As Prudence bathed, Gerty tried to distract herself by scrolling through her social media page. A notification from Vincent Kore popped up at the top of her screen. She quickly swiped it away.

Gerty was feeling frenzied. She wanted so desperately to talk to Prudence about what had happened. When she heard that Vincent had been suspended, and about the subsequent rumors regarding him and Prudence, she worried about her. Gerty didn't know if Vincent had taken advantage of her or how Prue felt, but she did notice a dramatic change in her behavior. Where Prudence had once been a confident and stoic force, she was now an empty shell with eyes that were constantly red from tears.

She wasn't reading anymore and wasn't eating—not even the roll that came with her dinner. Gertrude never would have thought that Vincent was capable of crossing a line like that and only hoped it had been mutual. Though the thought still lingered in her mind that maybe it wasn't.

Maybe the "milk incident" had to do with a different white liquid and was, in fact, a cover-up that allowed him to take advantage of Prue undetected. Gerty genuinely hoped that this wasn't the case. Vincent had reached out to her several days into his suspension, asking about Prudence, but Gerty didn't reply, too disgusted with the idea of what might have happened.

"Times up, here's your towel." Gerty handed Prudence the linen and shut off the water valve.

Prudence gingerly wrapped herself in the towel. "Gertrude—Gerty?"

Gerty's eyes searched her with concern as she met Prudence's gaze.

"Yeah, Prue?"

Tears welled up rapidly as a large bubble rose into Prudence's chest and throat. She couldn't speak, couldn't ask the question that had been burning a hole in her heart. She just sobbed and began crumbling to the floor. Gerty caught her before she met the ground and held her tightly. She rubbed Prudence's back affectionately as she cried into Gerty's chest.

"Oh, Prue. It's going to be ok."

CHAPTER 18

After a couple days of messages back and forth, and a thorough

background check performed by Emma's wife, Joy, Vincent was invited

to meet her in person. He set out early Saturday morning to Emma's

home, which happened to be the very same one she had lived in 12 years

prior. Vincent's palms remained sweaty the entire ride. His stomach

churned with nerves as he contemplated all the questions he wanted to

ask.

Emma, now in her 50s, seemed nice through their correspondence,

though Joy was undeniably wary of a strange man sending her wife a

message out of the blue regarding a decade-old closed double homicide.

Rightfully so, of course, and he had no problem answering her questions to put the ladies' minds at ease.

As he drove, Vincent's mind shifted to Prudence whom he was growing increasingly worried about. His two-week suspension was almost up and though he was dying to get back and see her, he knew that wouldn't be an option.

He spoke with Gallagher to gain some insight, asking if Benitez was keeping his hands to himself.

"After what happened to you, I don't think that's likely. But honestly, I don't know. I'm sorry, man."

Gertrude hadn't returned his calls or text messages. It was apparent that she was disappointed in him.

Again, rightfully so.

But hopefully this meant she was keeping more of a watchful eye over Prudence, which provided him with some comfort.

After a little over 5 hours on the road, Vincent finally pulled into Emma and Joy's driveway and made his way to the front door. Lining the stairs were bushels of beautiful, white flowering dogwood. Vincent noticed a sign at the top of their porch stairs that read "Unless You're A Girl

Scout, We Don't Want Any!" accompanied by an eye-catching wind chime adorned with iridescent oyster shells.

When Emma answered, he recognized her immediately. She was a short, round woman with cherry-red cheeks and white closely cropped hair.

"Hi, I'm Vincent Kore," he said, noticing Joy just past Emma, seated in a recliner in what he assumed was the living room. She leaned back to catch a glimpse of his large frame in the doorway. Her bulbous eyes peered at him over her spectacles.

"Yes, hello! Please come in," Emma said, turning to the side to allow him through.

Vincent walked past her and nodded politely at Joy, who nodded back before returning to her sudoku. He noticed a stack of worn puzzle books on the side table adjacent to her recliner. An avid player.

On the walls were more quirky signs similar to the one on the porch, accompanied by picture collage frames. The house smelt of toffee. It was quite welcoming and helped put Vincent's nerves at ease.

"Please, have a seat!" Emma motioned toward the couch. "I have some fresh coffee if you're interested."

"That would be great. It was a really long drive. I could use the pick-me-up," he said.

Emma waddled into the kitchen, the floor creaking as she went. Vincent

sank into the stale, floral-patterned couch in the living room, looking

around to further admire their array of knick-knacks. They had quite

the collection of movies shelved on either side of their television.

Limited edition collections of classics such as The Godfather trilogy and

the works of Sidney Poitier. There was a North Carolina state flag

framed above the television and an assortment of cuckoo clocks that

ticked in unison. In a corner of the room sat a record player on a wooden

stand stuffed with vinyls. Above it hung a Japanese ivy adorned with the

light that flooded from the window behind it. Books lined the built in

shelves that encased their fireplace. Titles such as "Beloved", "A Room

of One's Own" and "Go Tell It On The Mountain" caught Vincent's eye.

As his eyes wandered around the room they eventually landed on Joy

who was staring right back at him. Her scrawny body looked sunken in

her large chair, wiry fingers laced around her puzzle book. Vincent

smiled awkwardly.

Moments later, Emma returned with a cart in which an assortment of

sugars was packed into an ornate, crystal tumbler. It also held a carton

of half and half, a French press filled with steaming hot coffee, a blue

Danube saucer piled with Lotus Biscoff cookies, and two mugs placed neatly together. Vincent opted for the "Too Glam To Give A Damn" mug

and poured himself some coffee.

"Thank you very much," he said, taking a sip. "This is good stuff."

"Drink all you want," Joy chimed in unexpectedly, not looking up from

her puzzle. "It's some fad coffee our grandson brought over. Don't care

for it myself."

Joy had a twang that curled at the ends of each word she spoke—a soft

echo of what must have been a childhood spent in the South. Emma

playfully batted at Joy's shoulder, then took her mug and sat across

from Vincent in her own recliner.

"Have a cookie with it! They're absolutely delicious," said Emma,

grabbing two for herself and dunking them eagerly in the coffee.

Vincent took one of the cookies and bit it dry. Joy peered up at him again

from behind her spectacles. He felt nervous under her gaze. Cookie

crumbles littered his jeans.

"You never mentioned how exactly you know Prue." she said, her tone

flat.

Vincent cleared his throat. All of a sudden, his palms were sweaty again.

"We are friends."

Joy nodded, though it was clear she didn't believe him entirely. "I see. Is she in any trouble?"

Now the hairs on the back of his neck prickled. He wished he knew.

"She's in prison, for first-degree murder."

Emma's spoon clanked against the inside of her mug. Joy closed her puzzle book. The ladies let out a deep sigh in unison, looking at each other wearily.

"I've been worried about that girl since they sent her away. I'd always hoped she would be ok. You know, come out as 'ok' as someone like her can," Emma said.

Vincent's chest was tightening. "You mean after her parents' murders?"

"There was something off about those two," Joy said. "I don't even remember Lara being pregnant before Prue showed up."

"It's true." Emma leaned in and opened another sugar packet for her coffee.

"Like she wasn't showing or didn't leave the house much?" Vincent asked.

"No, I mean one day her stomach was flat as a board and then the next month she and Sam had a little chubby baby girl in their arms," Joy said.

Vincent was confused. "When was this?"

"It was late spring, '93 or '94. Can't remember the year exactly," Joy replied.

"Maybe they adopted her?"

"I don't know. Maybe. They never said anything about adopting, though," Emma said. "It would make sense, I guess, because when we first saw baby Prue, she had to have been six months old."

"What did you think at the time?" he asked.

He hadn't taken another sip of his coffee out of fear that it would further upset his stomach, which was folding over in knots. So many questions wondering who the Malkins got her from and why sprinted through his mind, but he knew they couldn't possibly know the answers to all of them.

"I really don't know. I guess I hadn't put much thought into it. Adoption does seem plausible, now that I think of it. Prue really didn't look like either of them, right Joy?" Joy shook her head no, shrugging as she did. "What were her parents like? Sam and Lara."

"Well, back then I thought they were alright, but in retrospect I can see how reclusive they were," Emma went on. "They kept to themselves, secretive even. We'd invite them over for barbecues and Easter Egg hunts, to get that little girl out of the house sometimes, but they'd

always decline. Every now and then, when Prue would step outside,

which was never alone, mind you, she kept her eyes on the ground. Just

the saddest-looking little thing."

Vincent was at the edge of his seat, elbows perched on his knees as he

listened.

"We thought maybe she was just quiet like her parents. Maybe she had

trouble making friends. We never saw other kids over there," Emma

went on.

"Did she ever speak to either of you?" Vincent asked.

"A few times, never anything engaging. She was sweet when we did

talk, though very polite. She sounded years older than she was."

Vincent smiled softly though his heart was full of sadness as he pictured

a young, defenseless Prudence. To be that young and trapped for so long

like she was. Her eyes were no doubt always pleading for help when they

met someone else's, unable to ask. The three of them sat in silence for a

moment, as if mourning the child Prudence once was. Emma sipped her

coffee a few times as she contemplated how to say what was going

through her mind.

"After the murders, when everything about what they had done to that little girl came to light...I wondered if they *bought* her."

Vincent's brow furrowed and he leaned in further, setting his now-cold mug of coffee back on the cart. . "What do you mean?"

"Like bought her...for sex." Emma's tone lowered as she spoke, "Child sex rings were being uncovered left and right during that time. I couldn't help but think they may have been involved in one."

"Nothing was ever proven as far as we know, but that seemed pretty likely to us," Joy said. Vincent was stunned. Sure these were just theories, assumptions really. But he began to wonder if there was any validity to it all.

"Who did she kill?" Emma finally asked now that Vincent's line of questioning came to a halt.

"Her landlady."

"A woman!" Joy chirped, "After all the horrible things men had done to her as a child she goes and kills a woman?"

Vincent shrugged, rubbing his hands together, "I assume it was a circumstance of being in the wrong place at the wrong time."

Then, abruptly, Emma shot up. "Oh! Before I forget."

She set her empty mug on the cart and walked toward the back of the house, out of sight. When she returned, she was carrying an envelope. It was yellow with age, but perfectly intact.

"Here." She handed it to Vincent. "When they cleared out the Malkins' home, several boxes of personal belongings were left by the curb for trash pick-up. I found those pictures in one and saved them."

Carefully, he opened the envelope. It hadn't been sealed, just tucked in. There weren't many photos, maybe five or six, but they were in great condition. He pulled out one that featured a baby that appeared to be a few months old.

The back of the photo read "Prudence Malkin, 1993."

"I had always intended to send them to her."

Later that night, after Vincent had returned to Maine, he took Brocc for a much-needed walk and fed him. The poor pup had been cooped up all day and was starving for attention. Once Brocc was snout deep in his food bowl, after at least 10 minutes of belly scratches post-walk, Vincent settled onto the couch with his laptop, a stout, and the photos of Prudence.

To Emma and Joy, it was most plausible that Prudence had been purchased on a black market of sorts, but Vincent wondered if she had simply been taken. In the search bar, he typed, "Missing Children 1993 United States." He found a helpful site that allowed him to filter through the thousands of results by typing in Prudence's specifics; gender, age, hair color, etc.

He contemplated including her name, but decided against it. If she had been kidnapped, he doubted her captors would have kept her birth name. The filter yielded several results as he scrolled through the photos of children, Prudence's baby picture in hand.

So many of these babies looked the same, it was hard to tell them apart aside from their clothing.

After 20 minutes of scrolling, he grew frustrated and decided to put down the laptop for a moment. Vincent took a long gulp of his beer and exhaled deeply, his eyes falling on Brocc, who was busy gnawing on a dried pig's ear.

"What am I even doing at this point?" he asked the unbothered pup. He scratched the back of his neck and felt his head swim a bit. Vincent hadn't eaten anything but the cookie Emma offered him and an unsatisfying convenience store hot dog. His empty stomach was absorbing the beer too quickly, so he decided to put his glass down on the coffee table. Next to his coaster sat the remaining photos of Prudence. He picked them up again and started looking through them, examining her features more closely. Then he saw something, but his eyes blurred at the tiny detail. Vincent blinked rapidly, then squinted, looking back at the photo.

Is that a birthmark?

He turned on the lamp next to him and looked again to make sure it wasn't a shadow or smudge, but it wasn't. Baby Prudence had a milk chocolate-colored birthmark roughly the size of an M&M on her temple. "Oh, fuck!" Vincent exclaimed. With a fresh dose of determination, he picked up his laptop again and started looking through the photos of missing children; this time looking for the mark. He hardly blinked, scrolling through dozens of babies. Finally, he came across a baby girl, missing since May 23rd of 1993, with a little M&M birthmark on her temple.

Vincent made a major break in the case. He imagined this must have been how the detectives on the Night Stalker case felt when they were able to match the killer's footprint at every crime scene.

Demi Callard from Newark, New Jersey.

Her parents were listed: Justine and Andres Callard.

Vincent gulped hard. "They're still looking for her."

It felt like hundreds of thousands of little needles were pricking his

skin. This was amazing news. The fact that they were still looking meant

Prudence hadn't been sold into some child sex ring. She was kidnapped

from parents who loved her and wanted her.

Who *still* loved her and wanted her.

CHAPTER 19

Edgar came in to relieve Gerty at around 7:20 pm.

"Hope I didn't miss any mental breakdowns!" He laughed.

Gerty shook her head now regretting having told him about the other day. "Try to be on time, Benitez. Wouldn't want to have to report you for being tardy all the goddamn time."

Edgar paused, his smug grin growing as he weaseled his way in between the counter and Gerty, getting far too close for her comfort.

He captured one of her loose red curls in between his fingers and twirled it, "Oh come on Dirty Gerty, that wouldn't be very nice."

"You're so gross."

She grabbed her belongings and headed out the door, Edgar giggled behind her.

Her phone had been buzzing incessantly in her pocket for the last hour, but she was unable to get to it. She was too preoccupied with comforting Prudence. All day, Gerty had tried to get her to talk about what was wrong, but Prudence wouldn't, or couldn't, say anything. Though several nurses had been by to perform their routine psychiatric evaluations on the inmates, Gerty made up her mind to request a nurse to evaluate Prudence again as soon as possible. That woman needed help and they were clearly dropping the ball if they hadn't concluded that she needed to be taken down to the psych ward by now.

When she got settled in her car, Gerty unlocked her phone to see what all the fuss was about. She had another missed call and several texts from Vincent. Annoyance heated her cheeks and the tips of her ears. Whatever he had done to Prue, she concluded it was bad. It was about time that she gave him a piece of her mind. Gerty touched the call-back button and put the phone to her ear.

Vincent picked up almost instantly. "Gerty! Thank you for returning my call!"

"Where do you get off asking about her? What did you do to her?" she erupted into the receiver.

"Prudence? Is she ok?" He sounded genuinely concerned, which threw her off guard.

"What—no! She's not eating or drinking *at all* and will hardly say a word! What the hell happened?"

"Oh no…" Silence fell between them for a moment as Gerty awaited a response that Vincent was trying to muster. He felt sick knowing his fears about Prudence had come true. Brocc's ears perked up at the sound of Vincent's sudden, quiet sobs. The dog immediately jumped on the couch to console him, pushing his head underneath his owner's hand. When he spoke again, the sound of Vincent's sniffling and the sorrow in his voice extinguished the heat in Gerty's face. "Please tell her I didn't abandon her. Please…"

Her heart sank. "I—I will, Vin."

He took a deep breath and said, "Edgar being there can't be helping if she's spiraling like this."

"Benitez? Why?"

"He's the reason she's in there, remember? He terrorizes her. Please keep an eye on her. I know you probably have been, but I just have to say

it for my own peace of mind." Vincent leaned forward on his knees,
rubbing the back of his neck.

Now Gerty felt regretful for not considering it was potentially Edgar
causing Prudence's mental state to decline. She would be certain to
mention it when she filed her request tomorrow. "I'm sorry I haven't
been texting you back. With you getting suspended and the way Prue has
been acting, I didn't know what to think."

"I get it, it's ok. It wasn't right for me to get so involved, but Prue...she
needs me." Vincent went on: "I really need a favor."

"What is it?"

"This won't make sense, and it might set her back too, but she needs to
know." In silent anticipation, waiting for him to speak, Gerty didn't
realize she was holding her breath. Vincent hated for it to be this way
but he had a feeling that he wouldn't get to Prudence fast enough to tell
her about what he had uncovered.

"Please tell her that the Malkins were not her parents."

Sitting up in her bed, leaning against the wall, a depleted Prudence
attempted to doze off. She hoped to trick an ever-watching Edgar into

believing she was awake so that she could get some sleep. Today had

been yet another emotionally overwhelming day and she needed the

rest if she could manage it.

Her hands rested palm side up on her knees, her head leaned against the

wall, and her shoulders were pulled down away from her ears. Her eyes

were closed softly as she pleaded with her mind to allow her peace.

Finally, her mind went blank. Her head fell slightly to one side as her

labored breathing caused her chest to steadily rise and fall, her heart

beating harmoniously with her breaths.

Vincent emerged in her mind.

His hand rose to her cheek, which fell instantly into his palm. Her eyes

burned in the presence of fresh tears, which he promptly wiped away.

Shivers traveled down her spine when she realized she could actually

feel him.

"Where have you been?" she cried, anchoring his hand to her face.

"I've missed you, Prue." His voice echoed in her mind.

Vincent cupped the back of her head, his fingers etching through her

hair, and pulled her into his chest. His scent was comforting and

intoxicating, like the first time he had embraced her. He was strong, but careful not to squeeze her weak frame too tightly. She missed him too; intensely and completely. The warmth of his chest sent a fire through her veins, every ounce of her being submerged in a warm bath of affection. She felt at home in his arms.

Edgar noticed her head fall as he watched Prudence on the surveillance screen. He chuckled under his breath, finding humor in her attempt to go unnoticed. He stretched his arms high and let out a sigh, then grabbed his baton and spun it in his palm as he stood. No woman, let alone some inmate trash, would brutalize and humiliate him and get away with it.

Edgar was determined to break her.

"Here comes your wake-up call, bitch!"

He practically skipped with glee as he made his way to Prudence's cell like a child rushing to the ice cream truck. He gripped the baton firmly and swung it hard at the window of her cell door, cracking the outer layer of plexiglass. Prudence woke with a jolt and fell out of her bed, hitting her head hard on the concrete floor.

Edgar bellowed a cheer. "And the crowd goes WILD!"

Prudence rubbed the fresh bump on her forehead and looked up at the cracked window. She charged up toward the door and screamed a blood-curdling cry.

"Oh-ho! She's alive! How goes it, Peaches? Are you a little grumpy?" Edgar condescended to her, his nose brushing against the window. "Did Daddy wake you too early?"

A faint voice from the neighboring cell called for him to leave her alone as other voices farther down erupted in laughter and cheers.

Prudence slammed her fists on the door. "What do you want from me?"

A grin, stretching from ear to ear, rested on Edgar's face as his hot breath fogged the window. This was the first time in the last couple weeks that she retaliated in any way.

He was fired up by the applause and Prudence's rage.

He wanted to take it a step further.

Edgar brayed a loud guffaw that was met with more excitement and jeering from the other inmates.

Prudence's stomach dropped as she watched his wild expression just through the glass. Her hands trembled sliding down to her sides.

She just needed him to stop.

She took several steps back and began to peel off her clothes. "Is this what you want, Edgar?" Her eyes glazed over, her heartbeat steadied. "A special show... just... for... you?"

His smile faded as he watched her breasts emerge from her bra. Her pants slid off her hips. The hunger in his eyes intensified as he gawked at her. Prudence kicked away the clothes and stood still, stark naked, beckoning for him to enter.

"What are you waiting for?" she asked in a breathy voice, her eyelids heavy, her lips pouting.

Edgar's eyes were hooded by a stern brow as he unlocked her door and stepped inside. Guarded with his baton firmly in hand, he walked around Prudence, looking her over, finally stopping behind her. Edgar reached his baton around and over her neck, pressing it lightly into her throat as a warning. He dug his fingers into her side.

"You need this cock again?" he spoke into her ear. His breath was nauseating.

She would give him what he wanted in hopes that he would back off. Maybe she could close her eyes and pretend he was Vincent until it was over.

Maybe everything would be ok.

Edgar forcibly kicked in her knees, causing her legs to buckle. Prudence knelt to the ground in front of him. He lowered himself with her.

"Tell me you need it." Edgar pushed, swiftly burrowing his nose into her neck. He sniffed deeply, her scent rousing him more. Prudence didn't flinch or wretch in disgust, though her insides crumbled. She had learned long ago to show no sign of discomfort or fear.

Tears formed in her eyes as the memories of the men who would come into her room at night rushed back to the forefront of her mind. A big, disgusting man towered over her and stripped off all of his clothes. Prudence was frightened and started to sob, knowing what was to come. He yelled at her for crying and kicked her in the stomach knocking the wind out of her. She wrapped her arms around her tummy, tears dripping from her chin as she gasped for air. He then picked Prudence up by her shoulders and threw her down onto the bed. Her favorite Strawberry Shortcake sheets wrinkled beneath them. Pinning her to the bed, he forced himself onto her. Father stood just outside the door, his feet blocking the hall light, listening. She was so small, the man was so heavy.

The pain.

The room started spinning making her dizzy. Her chest was tight, her breath shallow.

"You smell ripe, Peaches," Edgar grumbled before undoing his pants with his free hand, then stroking himself.

She could not do this. Would not do this.

Never again. Never ever again.

Edgar was so mesmerized by her bottom that he failed to notice Prudence slowly reaching up for the baton.

Hastily, she grabbed hold of it and ripped it clean out of his hand. He stumbled back. Just as he regained balance, Edgar attempted to lunge and tackle Prudence to the ground only for her to hit him fast and hard against the face with the baton.

He fell to the ground, disoriented, and tried to roll over to get back up. Prudence straddled him and struggled to pin his arms beneath her knees. He jerked against her hard, but she persisted, pushing all of her weight down onto him.

He snarled, calling her every obscenity he could conjure, threatening her and kicking his legs frantically.

Finally, he bucked her off him like a ferocious bull, throwing her across the room, causing her to drop the baton. A second after Prudence hit the floor, she was up and running back at him. They collided.

Edgar brutally punched her in the face, she instantly felt the skin below her eye rip open. She winced in pain. He then wrapped his hands around her neck and squeezed tightly, grunting and growling as he did. Prudence couldn't breathe. She choked, gasping for air as she tried in vain to pry his fingers from her throat.

She reached her hands up between his arms and found his face. She dug her nails into his eyes. He howled and wriggled in pain as she pushed him into the wall with all her might. With a jolt, he released her neck. She took hold of his head and beat it into the wall. Edgar crumbled to the floor, barely able to stay conscious when he caught one last glimpse at Prudence's frenzied, bloodshot eyes.

She retrieved the baton and slammed the butt of it into the bridge of his nose causing it to cave in. Over and over and over she hit him, completely pulverizing his face. Edgar's blood splattered all over her, trickling down over her stomach and pooling onto him. His body convulsed violently beneath her.

The ringing in her ears morphed into screams that came from the other women in their cells. They'd each pressed their ears against their doors, desperately trying to eavesdrop on the night's entertainment when the commotion began. Prudence looked up from Edgar's distorted, bloody face and saw that the door was slightly ajar.

Perfect.

She grabbed the keys from his belt loop, leapt up off of him, and walked out the door, her body vibrating all over. As she passed each cell door, Prudence looked into the windows to see the women's horrified expressions.

"Whore," she called out to one. "Bitch!" she called out to another.

"Slut! Tramp! Harlot! Jezebel!"

Prudence came upon the first door. Swinging the baton in hand, she unlocked it and walked inside.

"Hey girl, hey." Prudence jested. "Juarez, isn't it?" She asked, looking down at the cowering woman to the back of the cell. She had shoved herself beneath the sink.

"You got 15 years for solicitation of a child, right? *Your* child."

Juarez sobbed loudly, begging Prudence to leave her alone as she walked towards her.

Closing the space in between them.

Prudence grabbed her by the hair, Juarez kicked and pleaded. She threw her to the ground and swung the baton against her face.

Juarez let out a guttural cry.

Prudence shoved the baton in her mouth then jumped down on it hard, severing the woman's jaw from her skull.

Minutes later, she emerged, fresh blood dripping from her naked body. Her grin was so wide that her cheeks ached. She giggled as she opened the next door.

The clicking sound of her door unlocking evoked a bone-chilling scream from the woman within. But Prudence could no longer hear their screams, cries, or pleas. Just her song, swimming melodically through her mind as she bludgeoned each of them to death. It felt like she was the star of a Broadway show, executing its dramatic climax as she danced across the stage. Her body moved fluidly like silk in the wind.

Bell; 9 years for indecent acts with a minor.
Johnson; 28 years for possession of crack cocaine and endangering a minor.
Velasco; 20 years for the exploitation of a minor.

Covered in their hot, slick blood, Prudence made it to the last door, smearing the blood on her tummy with her hand like a lotion. She peeked inside, her eyes heavy with exhaustion, and saw Collins. She was kneeling in the corner at the back of her cell, crying silently.

Prudence's breaths were labored. She felt drained and heavy, squeezing the newly formed tension in her neck and shoulder.

Prudence wouldn't kill Collins.

She was a good mother.

She dropped the keys and baton as tears welled up in her eyes. She was done.

Collins heard the keys and the baton hit the floor. She looked up from beneath her arms and saw nothing in the window of her cell door. Slowly, she rose to her feet, shaking with fear as she did, and walked over to the door. Rising on her toes, she looked out the window and down at a figure curled up on the floor like an infant, painted a dark, crimson red.

Prudence was holding her knees to her chest, rocking herself gently, her eyes completely devoid of light. Collins' stomach churned at the sight of all the blood smeared up and down the hall. Tears streamed over her cheeks, bile built up in her throat. She wanted to speak to the fragile woman on the floor just outside to ask if she was ok, but she was too terrified that the demon would re-emerge.

Prudence's chest swelled, then sank as she let out a sorrowful, guttural scream. "Vincent!"

Vincent won't want you now, Prudence.

Monster.

Filth.

CHAPTER 20

June 2019

V incent couldn't bring himself to go to Edgar's funeral. He was by no

means happy that Edgar had died, but the array of feelings he was

having about *all* of it was crippling. Though Edgar was a deplorable man,

Vincent didn't think he deserved to die. Especially not in that way.

Edgar did, however, deserve to get fired or to serve time for his

mistreatment of the inmates.

Vincent couldn't help but think that if he, or anyone else, for that

matter, who knew what Edgar had been doing with the inmates, had

told the warden, Edgar would be in jail right now. The inmates and all

the other women he encountered would be safe from him and he would

be safe, too. From Prudence.

Prudence.

Vincent bowed his head, resting it in his hands. His heart was shattering for her. Knowing what he knew now, the anguish she must have felt, leading her to do what she did.

According to Fletcher, when he had come upon the scene early that morning, the stench of iron and death filled his nose. A copious amount of partially dried blood was streaked across the floor up and down the hall leading to the inmates' cells. Their doors were all wide open save for one. As he walked past each, he saw their remains inside, every woman bludgeoned to death with two exceptions: Collins, still locked up, and Prudence. She was curled up in her blood-stained sheets, Edgar lifeless on the floor of her cell. At first, he thought she was dead too on account of all the blood, but then he noticed her breathing.

For the last several weeks, she sat in a catatonic state in the psychiatric ward of the prison, not once speaking about the incident. Vincent was finally able to convince Seifert to allow him to see her.

He waited uncomfortably in his seat for the nurse to return and escort him back. Nerves were causing his leg to bounce uncontrollably. Guilt ran thick through his chest as he cursed himself for not speaking to Gerty hours sooner. Maybe if Prudence knew that he hadn't abandoned her, this wouldn't have happened. Maybe if she had known about her real parents. "Maybes" flew aimlessly throughout his mind like mosquitoes around a fluorescent light.

When Collins gave her account of what had happened that gruesome night, she said that Prudence had stopped when she came upon her cell. Collins didn't know why. She said that Prudence had dropped her weapon and cried hysterically for quite some time, screaming Vincent's name and muttering curses at herself.

"It wasn't right what happened to those girls," Collins said, "but it wasn't right what had been happening to Prue neither. I heard all the shit Benitez was saying to her, the way he was treating her. Like a damn dog. We all could hear it, but the others egged him on. Bunch of 'pick me' bitches. Then she just snapped. Can't say I blame her. It's fucked. It's all fucked."

On his shoulder, Vincent felt a tap that startled him. He hadn't even noticed the nurse who now appeared in front of him. "You can come back and see her now."

Prudence sat straight up in her bed facing the window. When she first arrived, it had been a shock to her system to see the sun again after well over a month in solitary. The rays of sunlight that beamed into her room enriched her cold, tired body. Though it wasn't enough to wake her from her ever consuming nightmare.

Prudence's right wrist was shackled to the bed frame. At this point, she was no longer a danger to anyone, but she understood the formality. Even she didn't trust herself. She felt numb, but not in the way that brought her comfort. She was completely depleted, her insides felt corroded as a rotted tree. Her heartbeat echoed pitifully within her empty chest.

Each day, she hoped it would just stop.

The nurse, whose name she hadn't bothered to remember, told her she had a visitor. Another doctor, most likely. Flashbacks of Dr. Taylor plagued her with every question they asked. And like she did with Dr. Taylor, she told them nothing. Her life came full circle again and again, it would seem.

In the back of her mind, she hoped it was Vincent who was waiting to see her out there, but her sad heart couldn't bring itself to flutter at the notion. Prudence was convinced she would never see him again.

"Prue?"

Her eyes widened at the sound of his voice. She turned around to see if it was really him and not a fantasy that her cruel mind was playing on her again. But sure enough, there he stood. He wasn't wearing the uniform she was accustomed to seeing him in. Instead, he wore slacks, chestnut dress shoes, and a white button-up shirt that suited him very nicely. She choked on her words as they tumbled out of her mouth. "Why are you here?" she asked.

"I wouldn't have left you if I had a choice."

His hands were clammy, clasped together behind him, and his legs quivered. Even now—though the color of her skin had paled, her eyes were sunken from lack of sleep, and her body appeared to be more fragile than ever—she was still so beautiful. His desire to cloak her in affection and be her sanctuary intensified at the sight of her.

"May I?" He gestured to a spot on the bed beside her. She nodded her approval, so he sat down, sinking into the mattress. He was grateful she had a comfortable bed compared to those elsewhere in the prison. Vincent took her free hand in his and squeezed it affectionately. He was pleased when she squeezed back.

"How are you?"

Prudence sighed and brought his hand up to her face. He caressed her cheek just as he had in her dream.

"I'm not well. I haven't been well for a very long time," she said, sniffing as she did. "Did you lose your job because of me?"

"No, I was suspended, but not because of you, Prue. I made the choice to get that close. But I'm glad I did." Vincent gave her a small smile. "I think it might be time I reconsider my career choice anyway. I can't continue to work here if it means I can't see you."

Prudence looked up at him now. His beard and hair were freshly trimmed and he smelt of warm vanilla. She felt at ease next to him and dreaded the moment when his visit would inevitably come to an end. But she was confused about why he had come back to her after learning what she was and what she had done. She couldn't understand why he bothered caring about her at all.

"Did they send you in just to get me to talk?" she asked, taking back her hand and tucking it under her thigh.

Vincent considered his answer for a moment. "They didn't send me, I asked to come. They do want you to talk, but it doesn't really matter to me what they want at this point. I won't try to make you say anything you don't want to say."

Prudence paused for a moment, grief and happiness playing a close game of tug of war in her mind. Finally, she began. "I didn't want to kill all those women. I lost complete control after I killed Edgar and was unable to stop until my body was completely spent."

"Collins said that the others were provoking him," Vincent said.

"Yes...I needed it all to stop. I can't go on like this anymore. My mind and body can no longer withstand it. I just want to end it all..."

Vincent brought his hand up her back and rubbed it gently. "I don't think that's the answer, Prue. The best people to talk to about what you're going through, that can understand and help you, are these doctors. I believe you can get better."

She shook her head in disbelief. "Why aren't you scared of me, Vincent? You shouldn't be here."

He sat still for a moment, sighing heavily through his nose. "You know, I'm not sure what I'm supposed to feel about this. What you've done is fucking terrifying, and I can't understand it for the life of me, but I'm trying. It's not clear what the future holds, especially now." He felt frustration bubbling in his gut so he took a deep breath before continuing. "I've told myself to leave you alone, that this isn't something I can handle. But I do know, beyond all of the fear and uncertainty, that I *care* about you and I want to be there for you." He looked at her for a response, but she froze. He reached for her hand again. She let him take it, sparing a glance at their fingers intertwining. Vincent brought her hand up to his lips and kissed it gently. "I've spent so much time fighting how I feel and questioning myself, but I can't question that. And yeah, I am scared, but not of you. Underneath it all, Prue, you're so much more than a broken thing. I can see that. You're resilient, smart…charismatic as hell and a little funny at times. Even though I was so fucking mad, I had to laugh after that shit you pulled with the milk cartons. You deserve someone to be there for you, to be in *your* corner for a change. "

Prudence was shocked and didn't know what to say. She felt like the right thing to do would be to discourage his sentiments and tell him to run. Tell him he deserved better and to not waste his time any longer on a wretch like her.

What could I offer him?

"And there's something I think you deserve to know," Vincent said, reeling her back in. He turned to face her. Brushing a stray curl behind her ear, Prudence searched his eyes.

"The Malkins were not your parents." Vincent continued to hold her

hand reassuringly as she tensed up. "I visited an old neighbor of yours

and—anyway, I know this is a lot, but I was able to find them."

"Find who?" Prudence asked, she grew anxious.

"Your real parents."

Prudence pulled away from him. "How do you know for sure?"

Vincent reached into his back pocket and removed a folded piece of

paper and a single photo. He handed her the photo first. Quickly, she

recognized it as a photo of herself as an infant. Then Vincent carefully

unfolded the piece of paper and handed it to her as well. It was a missing

persons flyer with the name Demi Callard written under a photo. The

photo, she realized, was of her.

All this time.

It almost made sense now, why Mother and Father could do what they

did to her. She had always thought something was fundamentally wrong

with her for her parents to abuse her the way they did. Allowing men to

rape her and beat her. Allowing them to use her like a rag only to doll

her back up afterward and throw her to someone new. They didn't love

her, they never had.

Vincent sat in silence as Prudence read the flyer, his hand resting on her

shoulder. She read her parents' names again and again until they were burned into her brain. Perhaps it was a subconscious effort to erase the Malkins.

Justine and Andres.
Justine and Andres.
Callard.

"My name is Demi Callard?" she asked, looking up at Vincent. He smiled and nodded. "*My* name is Demi."

This changed everything. No longer was she some vile creature borne from monsters incapable of caring about their own spawn, undeserving and incapable of love. She was a lost child searching for purpose, confined to a life of misery. She wanted to meet her real mother and father. *Mom and Dad.* She wanted to be their little Demi again.

But how could she?

Prudence didn't know what was in store for her after what she had done. She was terrified, but knew she had to do things differently from now on. For herself.

"That flyer is yours to keep if you decide you want to reach them. The number to get in contact with them is there at the bottom."

She folded it back up with her picture inside, then set it down beside her.

"Thank you. My gratitude for all that you've done for me and shown me is immeasurable. I can't even begin to express it." She bowed her head, fighting the encroaching cloud of shame that hovered over her at all times. "I have a very deep regard for you as well, Vincent."

Just then a knock came on the door. Startled, they both looked back to see the nurse standing in the doorway, her arms crossed and lips pursed.

"Time's up," she said before stepping back out.

Vincent leaned in and kissed her on the cheek, then lingered, their faces pressed together. She didn't want him to go or for their time together to end. She ran her fingers through his beard, tracing his jaw with her thumb.

"Will I see you again?" she whispered.

"Very soon, Demi."

CPSIA information can be obtained
at www.ICGtesting.com
Printed in the USA
BVHW042053010821
613371BV00009B/116

9 780578 961460